Alternative Apocalypse

Edited by
Debora Godfrey and Bob Brown

Cover Design
Debora Godfrey

Published by

B Cubed Press
Kiona, WA

Copyright© 2019 B Cubed Press
Interior Design (ebook) Bob Brown
Interior Design (print) Bob Brown
Cover Design Debora Godfrey
Print ISBN- 978-1-949476-08-8
Electronic ISBN 978-1-949476-09-5
First Printing 2019
First Electronic Edition 2019

Copyright

Introduction

Thanks all. An Apocalypse is always a challenge and so was this book. So many great stories, enough for three books and we had to choose. While our names are on the cover as editors, this would not have been possible without the other souls, who read stories and helped us through the decision making processes. Impossible without the tireless enthusiasm and recommendations from Rebecca Mcfarland Kyle and other readers, a team that will be employed more efficiently in the future. Thank you Shelby Gremel, the ever wonderful Wondra Vanian, Charles Boyd, and Susan Murrie Macdonald who helped read through the stories. And a special thanks to Ben Howels, our fabulous proofer.

But mostly to the writers. You glorious souls who labor to perfect your vision and then subject it to the whims of editors and eventually the public where your soul is laid bare as you put forth your best for their judgment and wait, like actors on an extended stage, for the opening night reviews to roll in. Without you, we are nothing and to you, all of you in the book or not, we owe our gratitude both as publishers and readers.

As a note, this is an international edition with writers from all over the globe, even Texas. For that reason we've left the English spellings for works from those parts of the world. Sometimes it's best to let the words of the authors speak.

Thank you all, and now, on with the Apocalypse.

Bob Brown and Debora Godfrey

Table of Contents

The End of the World

J. J. Steinfeld

And when the world does end
as it surely will, place your bets,
either in cataclysm or listlessness
I wonder who will hit the final home run
in the bottom of the ninth
or who will sink the final free throw
in a schoolyard game
where winning isn't everything
who will write the final poem
in ink or blood or dancing electrons
last painting or nearly last
a few more brushstrokes
almost capturing the beauty of sanctity
last story, last novel, last kick at the can
sing the final song
off key or mellifluously
and at the end
what inspiration will there be?

All those obits left unwritten
all those apologies left dangling in the air
and desperate prayers not quite right or finished
all those acts of contrition unperformed
pleas for forgiveness unarticulated
not enough time
never enough time
especially at world's end.

Alternative Apocalypse

The Deserter

Jim Wright

Once, long ago in arrogant youth, I attempted to wage war on God.

For this foolishness, I was cursed—or perhaps granted a boon, depending on how you look at things.

And now? I know things. This knowledge comes not in the usual manner of human knowing. I just know things, the past, sometimes the future, and always the terrible present. I don't know how I know, or why—the purpose of it, the principles of it, those things are a million years beyond human comprehension.

I just know.

I heard them long before the sound of their march reached the meadow.

"Someone's coming," the young man said. Michael. I only remembered because it was unusual. Nowadays people in this part of the world generally don't name their kids for archangels.

"Soldiers," I told him.

"Bloody USA." Michael spat on the ground, then added reflexively, "No offense."

I shrugged. Bloody was hardly the worst thing I've heard my nation called.

"There's a warship arrived in Whittier. These ones, they come through the tunnel a week ago and they've been swaggering around Anchorage like they still own the place."

"You might have mentioned it earlier. For politeness sake, I mean."

"Sorry. I was...well." Contrite, he clutched the shrunken bundle in his arms tightly. "You're not surprised?"

I shrugged, what was there to say? I know things. I knew when they left the ruins of Tijuana Antiguo, sailing up the coast through the Inland Passage. I knew when they left

Anchorage and started up the mountain. I'd known Michael was coming too, long before he himself did.

"Maybe you should..."

"You can't hide from your fate, son. Church Intelligence knows I'm here. I always knew they'd come for me—sooner or later. We are each granted free will. But the choices we make, or don't make, always come round in the end. My destiny hasn't been my own for a very long time."

He opened his mouth to argue, but I cut him off. "We don't have much time. Tell me about your daughter."

He really didn't have to say anything. I could see it in the little girl's sallow sunken skin, in the wispy remnants of her blond hair, in her bruised hopeless eyes watching listlessly from the blanket—leukemia.

"Give her to me."

"We tried everything." He handed the child to me, she felt like a bundle of sticks, dry and weightless. "Chemo. Radiation. Hell, even *prayer*." He spat into the grass again. Unlike the USA, there weren't many believers left in Alaska. He must have been truly desperate to hike up here from the city to beg a cure from me of all people.

"And now you need a miracle."

He nodded his head, shamefaced.

So I gave him one.

A genuine miracle. I put my hand on his daughter's fevered cheek and the power flowed through my fingers. My vision dimmed to near black. There was pain, a moment of light and warmth, and it was done.

My vision was darkness and fireflies, but I could still hear the hum of servos, the muted clank of ceramic armor, the tread of heavy boots. They were here.

"You there!" A familiar haughty Southern drawl from the edge of the clearing. Vision was coming back, but I couldn't see that far yet. I didn't have to. I knew. No magic. No divine knowledge. No, I knew that voice.

And, of course it would have to be him. Of course.

Funny, my gift hadn't seen fit to warn me about that. God is an iron.

And worse.

"You're the faith healer?" the voice demanded.

I handed the girl back to her father. Her skin was already turning pink.

"Is she...?" His voice was terrible with hope.

"Go."

"I can pay a little."

"Go. *Now.*"

Miracles leave me weak and shaky, hypoglycemic. They must have forgotten to mention that, back when they were writing the holy books. I don't understand how it works, no one does, but even angels can't change physics. It's basic thermodynamics: the energy must come from somewhere. So, I sat on the steps of the cabin and ate bread and cheese and waited.

My vision cleared, the day turned bright again.

And the meadow was filled with a company of hard young men and women in lightweight power armor, the Golden Cross and the Lone Star on their chests.

The Major stopped at the foot of the steps, right hand resting suggestively on his holstered pistol.

It was him. I'd know him anywhere. He looked just like his father.

I might have said many things. "Hello, Diego," seemed the safest.

He stood, head cocked to one side, and regarded me intently. He was taller. Filled out. When last I'd seen him, he'd had two bright brown eyes surrounded by warm brown skin. Now the right eye was milky white like a boiled egg and flanked by thick scar tissue which trailed down his neck into the high uniform collar. An energy weapon had brushed across his face once. Men generally do not survive a fight with angels. He'd gotten lucky.

"My God, it *is* you." His voice was thick and filled with gravel.

I'd changed too, far more than he had. Old and gray and twisted by the years, and the outside was nothing compared to the changes within. He almost stepped forward, as if to touch my shoulder. And for a moment I thought he actually would. I could see his muscles tense and relax, tense and relax, and his armor servos rustled with indecision.

"I thought it must be you, from the reports, the rumors down in town," he growled like boulders rubbing together; he must have breathed flame once. "I prayed I was wrong."

The Church hadn't seen fit to warn him in advance either and we are all pawns of capricious powers in our own ways.

"You're a long way from Dallas, son."

"Yes, *Captain*," he snarled, coming down hard on my former rank. "We are a long way from home. So are you."

"It's good to see you, Diego. Really, I mean that. You have no idea how much." And I truly was, though it filled me with sadness knowing what was to come. I didn't need God's prescience to see that. "I don't suppose I could convince you to take your soldiers and your ship and leave while you still can?"

"Not a chance" he answered contemptuously. "I am not you." The righteous fire of conviction burned in his one good eye, just as it had once burned in mine. "You, what? Quit? Deserted? Became a, a, a *witch doctor?*"

"Technically the term is 'Virtue,' but witch doctor will do. 'Faith healer' is closer."

"So, you 'heal' the sick and the lame." He spat again. "How noble. They worship you here, do they?"

"Worship? Hardly. And nobility has nothing to do with it."

These northerners, they hike, limp, ride, and crawl up the path from Anchorage stepping in moose shit all the way, and come to me because, like the young parents now hurrying away down the trail to town, they are desperate. Religion and science had failed them. All they had left was...me.

"Where are your men?" he looked around the clearing, as if he expected to find them hiding among the fireweed.

"Dead, most of them." I'd arrived the same way he had, years ago, wearing the same uniform. And I faced the same choice he would soon. In the end, it's always about choices. And the consequences, of course. "The rest? Well, like me, it's complicated."

He wasn't interested in complications. "We're here to finish your mission."

"Of course you are."

"We're going to kill the demon. And *you*," he said, stroking his pistol, "you're going to show us the way."

✳✳✳

They had a mule.

They must have badgered somebody out of it in Anchorage. Maybe they paid for it; gold isn't as valuable here as it is in Texas, but we'll take it in trade. The machine was nearly as old as I am. The paint was chipped and the Boston Dynamics logo had faded to near illegibility. It was bent and battered, patched with duct-tape, scarred by weapons fire. It tended to list slightly to starboard. Its power-plant wheezed like a dying thing, but it plodded gamely over the broken asphalt and followed the soldiers like a faithful hound. Our packs were lashed to its cargo frame.

Clumsy and arthritic as the machine was, I wished I was half as spry.

"You can't witch-doctor yourself?"

"No," I admitted. Miracles don't work for the miracle worker. I never asked why. Given human nature, the reason seemed obvious.

Diego snorted in disbelief, not that I couldn't heal myself, I suspected, but at the idea I might be able to heal anybody.

"What happened to you?"

I had to step carefully on the rough trail. In the early days of the Dark Rapture, something massive had smashed down from the heavens into the Knik Arm. Shock waves from the impact had shattered the road to rubble. The blast leveled much of Anchorage and the surrounding communities. The fault lines had let go all at once. The ground quaked and the seas rose and the angels followed and the interior of Alaska became dangerous to men—or more dangerous depending on your point of view.

"Every action has a reaction, Diego. They sent me to kill God. This is the result."

"And you're not going to try and stop me from the same?"

"We make our own fate, son," I said.

"Bah!" he sneered, angry and righteous. "The truth is you failed and didn't have the guts to face the consequences. So, you hid out here in this wilderness peddling snake oil and left your family to pay for your failures."

"I won't deny it," I shrugged.

There wasn't any point in denying it. You can't reason with fanatics.

Especially when they're right.

"Tell me about the demon," he demanded as we climbed over rubble and waded through chest high alders.

Wheels within wheels turned in my mind's eye, "I can't describe it. It's like nothing you can imagine."

Diego snorted in contempt. "I've faced the Fallen. I don't have to imagine anything." His scarred armor flashed dully in the sunlight and the servos hummed with power. His hand traced the contours of the assault carbine slung across his chest; the weapon's grips were black and worn from heavy use. He was confident and experienced, but then you don't make major any other way.

It's also why the army went through a lot of majors.

"Cherubim," I nodded. "Foot soldiers, I'd guess. Since you still have most of your face."

He touched the scars beneath his ruined eye, realized he was doing it and angrily snapped his hand away. "The army of lesser Fallen during the Great Withdrawal. After they salted Chicago. *This*," he touched his face again and said with bitter pride, "was a seraph."

"This is different, Diego. As powerful as a seraph is, an army of cherubim, this is like nothing you've ever seen."

He snorted in disbelief, but his brow furrowed. We walked in silence for a hundred steps—silence except for my ragged breathing. I was old, old and in no shape for a forced march into the badlands.

"Tell me what's ahead."

No one comes this far out from Anchorage, except for the foolhardy and the desperate. This used to be some of the most fertile land in Alaska. On the whole continent, in fact. I pointed to the blasted landscape, the smashed mountains rising to our right. "Now, well. We'll have to cross the flats, there's a river but it should be low enough to wade across this time of year. There are some ruined towns. Then a road that used to lead up to a park and over a pass down into a long valley. There were mines there once, gold mostly. Before. Now it's filled with Constructs. Like those in the Midwest. Whatever they were doing, they wanted something in that valley. The complex is mostly dead now, abandoned. Very, *very* dangerous. If you go in, you'll never come out. If you stay too long, you'll get sick...or worse. Your armor won't protect you from it. The locals call it The Blight. Just over the pass, before you reach the first of the fairy towers, there's a box canyon and an old mine. It's there."

"There will be guardians."

"Giants. In the pass."

"Nephilim," he spat in disgust. "They'll have an archangel in command too."

He went forward to speak to his men.

I watched him go with some sadness. He'd always been a hard, incurious boy, proud and sure of himself. Once upon a time I thought that a virtue. Time and holy war, it seemed, had turned his confidence into bitter arrogance. It made me sad for the things that might have been.

The soldiers marched on, tireless in their youth and power armor. I lagged further and further behind with the baggage. They'd make camp at the river or in the ruins ahead and I'd catch up. Another day would see us to the Pass. My gift told me nothing of what would happen then.

"Pardon me," said the mule. "May I ask a question?"

I jerked around to stare in surprise at the machine and tripped over shattered pavement. One of the mule's actuators flashed out to steady me.

"You're self-aware?" Talking machines were uncommon these days and full artificial sentience even less so— particularly around those who still had Faith.

"'The better part of Valour 'tis Discretion,'" said the machine. "'In the which better part, I have sav'd my life.'"

"Beg pardon?"

"Shakespeare. Henry IV, Part I," the mule explained, aiming an optical sensor in my direction. "Advanced Capability Autonomous Support System (Experimental), Unit M3A21, United States Navy Development Group. Basically, I am an upgraded Army squad logistics robot designed for SEAL team support. Most of my comrades were lobotomized by zealots such as your friend, the major. It would seem human religion and artificial intelligence are not compatible. As such, pretending to be a simple brainless grunt was the prudent course of action."

"I see. Why reveal yourself to me?"

"A calculated risk. Curiosity. Conversation. Self-preservation." If the machine could shrug, I suspect it would have. "You can predict the future?"

"Yes. No. I see...what they choose to reveal to me. Possibilities. Choices. I just know things."

The machine mulishly persisted. "How does it work?"

I stopped for a moment, standing on a high slab of smashed concrete, the remains of a highway overpass. I could see Diego and his men half a kilometer ahead. He glanced over his shoulder, and then turned to continue on without pausing. A deliberate insult. He'd been mad at me for a long time. The current situation was unlikely to change his attitude.

"I have no idea. What do you know of angels?" I asked.

Fifty odd years ago, a new star rose in the east. It looked like a nearby nova, but of course it wasn't. It was too close, somewhere in the Oort cloud, some ways beyond Pluto.

A previously unknown astrophysical phenomenon, that's what the headlines called it.

A day later exotic energy and strange radiation sleeted down from the heavens, auroras flamed across the night skies in blazing curtains, and every unhardened electronic circuit in the world died—along with tens of thousands of people who depended on those machines.

Science speculated wildly about wormholes and dark matter and colliding micro-black holes.

Religion speculated wildly about a Second Coming and the End of Days and the Rapture.

The tinfoil hat crowd speculated wildly about aliens and Chariots of the Gods.

It may be they were all correct, or none of them. A half century and the destruction of half the planet haven't done much to improve human understanding.

As the machine spoke in quiet measured tones, I remembered the panic of that time. Half the world had gone dark and cold, the night skies were on fire, and somewhere up there a gateway had opened.

Then the angels appeared.

Renaissance artists painted them as handsome winged men, and that's the image I had in my own head before they arrived. But the ancient holy books described angels *far* differently, and those were the voices we should have listened to.

They were powerful beyond imagination, and far more terrible than anything described by religion.

Ancient text called them the Fiery Ones, and fiery they were.

And they were most certainly not men, handsome or otherwise.

"'Upon it stood the seraphims: the one had six wings, and the other had six wings: with two they covered his face, and with two they covered his feet, and with two they flew,'" the mule quoted Isaiah.

"Energy fields," I answered.

Wings of light and a thousand unnamed colors and terrible, terrible heat. Weapons, shields, transportation, life support, incomprehensible, magical, those wings are impossible to describe. Most humans alive today have never seen a seraph. Video and digital photography show only shifting light, impossible to focus on—the mechanical senses of machines like those of the mule were blinded by angels. The human eye, squinted nearly closed against the fire, sometimes sees structure within the light, a shadow of something strange and inhuman. Other instruments, when they worked at all, recorded electromagnetic flux and a ravening vortex of exotic particles.

"Cherubim are easier to see."

And even harder to describe as a result. Energy wings, roughly man-shaped, something that might be a head with a thousand shifting faces—some vaguely human, many not.

Soldiers, officers, workers, aliens, the many hands of God? No one knew.

"You were like them once," the mule said, waving an actuator towards the soldiers ahead of us. "A soldier. Rumor in Anchorage is that you can perform miracles now. In the meadow where we first met, leaving your home I saw a child healing from an incurable disease. I think the rumors must be true."

I shrugged. What was there to say?

"Are you still a Believer?"

"Gravity doesn't care if you believe in it. It'll kill you just the same."

"I don't understand."

"What I believe is that it doesn't matter," I answered truthfully, picking my way over the broken ground. It wouldn't do to twist an ankle out here.

"So, you have lost your faith."

"You misunderstand," I corrected the mule. "It's just the opposite. I have plenty of faith. Like the old song says, I've lost my *religion*."

"How can you have faith without religion?"

"Two thousand years of human development since last they came. Two thousand years. From their perspective, it's *nothing*. To them, to beings so fantastically advanced, the difference between our Bronze Age and our Information Age is *nothing*. They must be millions of years beyond us. To such creatures, two millennia of technological advance is so slight as to be undetectable. We can no more understand what they are than an ant can comprehend a quantum computer and, in fact, to them a flint hand ax and a thinking machine such as yourself are the same. Ants and human beings are the same. And these creatures? These angels? If we understand anything about them at all it's that they are only agents of something greater. Something up there." I gestured to the sky. "Something as far beyond them as they are beyond us. Whatever that is, if it's not *God*, it may just as well be."

"Others have said similar things," the machine acknowledged, sounding disappointed. "You said that you 'know things.' I wish for more information. I desire certainty. Proof. I can't help it. Part of my job was intelligence gathering. I was designed this way."

"I know things," I said to the mule. "I was *redesigned* this way. By them. Unfortunately, I can't offer you any proof. Only faith. And I can only tell you what they choose to tell me."

The machine was silent for a hundred steps. Thinking, I guess. We plodded along through the weeds and the dust and over the shattered concrete.

"'Neither let there be found among you any one that shall expiate his son or daughter, making them to pass through the fire: or that consulteth soothsayers, or observeth dreams and omens, neither let there be any wizard',," it said finally. "Your prescience is blasphemy to the major and his men."

"Oh yes indeed," I laughed. "They are Fundamentalist Christian Soldiers of the United States Ascendant. True believers. Likely they'll kill me before this is over."

If the Holy Books are accurate even in the most general sense, two thousand years ago angels took at least some passing interest in humanity. Maybe even a direct hand in our development. Or maybe we're remembering it wrong. This time it was different. Maybe we were different. Maybe they were different, a different group, some thought enemies of the previous ones—if concepts like friend and enemy even apply to such beings. I don't know. They appeared and did what they did and took no more notice of us than men fighting a war take of rats on the battlefield.

It wasn't God-like malice, it was supreme indifference.

If we figured into their plans in any fashion, then it was only as a footnote, the way a man might add a birdbath to his garden as part of a larger design.

"Fundamentalists like Diego," I told the machine, "they're traditionalists, hardliners who believe in the first two Testaments of the Christian Bible and not the Third one. Their religion will not allow them to believe they are so insignificant in the eyes of their God. They see all of this," I swept my arm across the blasted landscape, "as a lie. *The Lie*. They believe these angels are Fallen, enemies of Heaven. Maybe they're right. Maybe not. But, Diego and his men, and the nation that sent them, they believe they are fighting the final War against Evil itself."

"How do you know?"

"Because I used to believe exactly as they do."

"What changed?"

"Likely you'll see for yourself tomorrow."

"If these creatures are to humans as humanity is to ants," the machine asked slowly, "how does the major expect to defeat one?"

"He doesn't. But he reasons even ants can drive a man from a picnic."

✳✳✳

"Warning!" hissed the mule.

Diego's arm flashed out and the soldiers became statues.

My gift told me nothing. I know what they choose to tell me and they tell me nothing of themselves. Whatever waited ahead, it was in my blind spot.

I peered into the mist and saw only a mosaic of faint gray shapes. I could smell water. There had been a lake near the summit of the pass, we must be close.

There was a faint humming as the mule extended a mast, a bulb on the end opening like a flower to reveal a compact sensory array of crystal lens and fractional millimeter antennas.

Diego called softly to his point man, a single sharp syllable.

The scout crouched, peered into the fog and flashed a hand sign. Nothing. He dropped a HUD over his eyes and his helmet swiveled slowly back and forth. Dark steep slopes loomed on either side, huge boulders bulked faint in the thick mist, the perfect chokepoint. The soldier signaled again. Still nothing.

"Support?" Diego queried.

"Hot spots. Energy point sources. Increase in exotic particle count," the robot-mule reported. Its voice was flat and deceptively machinelike, devoid of intelligence.

"Range?" Diego demanded.

"Indeterminate," the mule answered. "Movement ahead. Assessment: possible ambush."

"Scout?" Diego checked again.

"I got nothing but fog, Sir. Nothing on HUD or the Mark I eyeball neither."

Lightning strobed and the fog turned brilliant white.

"*Hear me!*" The voice boomed like thunder and rolled down over the soldiers. They dropped without orders and scattered with practiced speed, going to cover among the rocks on either side of the trail.

In a few seconds, Diego stood alone in the pass, feet spread wide, fearless and gray in the mist. "I hear you."

"I am Zaphrael!"

"Support! Locate!" Diego commanded.

A ranging laser flashed out from the top of the robot's sensor mast, spearing over Diego's shoulder and pointing into the fog. "Zero degrees relative. Directly ahead."

Something man shaped separated from the fog and stepped soundlessly forward to block the trail.

Zaphrael. An archangel. A different one than the last time I'd been this way, naturally, since that one was dead. They didn't last long.

"Turn back," the archangel commanded. Its voice hurt my ears.

Once when I was a kid, I saw one of those nature shows. Baby birds, endangered California condors, raised in a laboratory breeding program. Human contact would damage their minds in ways that couldn't be undone. To keep the chicks from imprinting on humans, the scientists constructed a fake mother condor, a puppet of wire and foam and salvaged condor feathers, lifeless glass buttons for eyes and a plastic beak. It didn't look particularly convincing to me, but somehow the baby birds never saw the scientist's arm inside. Their simple bird brains could not pierce the facade or conceive of the intelligence and civilization beyond it—not even when they caught a glimpse of the lab technicians working behind the curtains.

"Abomination," I heard Diego hiss. The faint click-click of safeties disengaging came from the fog on either side of the road like the chirping of insects.

The archangel raised its arm, it held a horn. "Turn back. This place is not for your kind."

And the mist thinned to reveal massive shapes waiting silently on the slopes above the road. They weren't boulders after all.

"Giants," the mule whispered to me. We were far enough downslope not to be heard.

In ancient Jewish text, Nephilim were the result of a mating between the "sons of God" and the "daughters of men." Somehow, I doubt angels have anything like human DNA nor would they find human woman sexually arousing even if they did. These giants had been men once. *My* men, some of them, changed now into monsters, not quite gods, and perhaps those old descriptions weren't entirely wrong after all.

"Diego," I called. "Listen to him. Turn back, or this will happen to you."

Of course he ignored me.

Zaphrael stepped fully clear of the fog and stopped a dozen meters in front of Diego. The archangel appeared as a large powerfully built man--which would follow since First Sergeant Korpinski had been exactly that. White light flowed like robes, or wings, around him. And like the Nephilim, he too had been changed, raised from the dead and rebuilt into something terrible.

"Turn back!" Thunder crashed and Zaphrael lifted the horn. Its interior was infinity and dreadful dark light swirled in its throat.

Huge shapes moved ponderously downslope, barely seen through the fog.

Diego raised his weapon. "We will not!"

The archangel looked over Diego's shoulder. I thought of wire and foam with a man's skin and muscle stretched over it, animated by clockwork and the hand of God inside pulling the strings. It looked like a man, but nothing human remained. Its dark eyes met mine and suddenly the gift unfolded in my mind, branching probabilities, twisting futures, blood and fire and suns and stars and inevitable fate.

I opened my mouth to shout warning—but it was already far too late.

Diego barked a single sharp syllable and weapons roared in the mist. A rocket streaked out of the fog and exploded somewhere far upslope. Then another.

It's always about choices, and it had been a long time since Diego's fate had been his own.

I saw him go to one knee, head down on the stock of his carbine. The muzzle of his weapon flashed in controlled staccato bursts.

The archangel began to burn with terrible fire. Energy swirled like vast wings. Zaphrael swept the great dark horn across the pass and the world split asunder with the fearsome sound of it. The very air tore itself apart and the walls came down as stone shattered and the ground shook.

Then giants bounded from the fog into the rock field.

And men began to scream.

Diego was firing at point blank range, or near enough, and for a moment it appeared he might take down the archangel. It was possible, Korpinski and I had done it near this very same spot. For all the good it had done either one of us.

Diego wasn't as lucky, or as fast, or as good as we had once been.

I watched as the horn swept over him and he fell, crumpling into a broken heap on the side of the road. Zaphrael stepped over his body, glanced at me for a moment with black bottomless eyes, without recognition, without pity, without humanity, and then followed the giants into the fog.

The sound of battle retreated downslope.

The mule retracted its mast, armor plates snapped up like porcupine quills. It snatched at my arm with an actuator and tried to drag me towards cover. "This way!"

I know things. I don't know how I know, or why, I just do. I knew what had to be done.

"No." I pulled free of the machine and began walking upslope. "That's not how this ends. Come on."

He was still breathing when I reached him.

I took his head in my hands and the power flowed through my fingers. The pain came in waves of light and heat. It went on for a long, long time. I could feel the broken bones straighten, and the sound of flesh moving. The smell of raw lamb and charred meat faded.

I felt him *change*.

Then weakness washed over me in waves, the sounds of battle were lost in the buzzing roar and my vision dissolved into blackness and swirling sparks and the world went far away.

For a while, blessedly, I knew nothing.

✳✳✳

"Wake up." I felt the mule's actuator shaking me insistently. "Wake up."

The world came back into focus too far above the ground. After a moment, I realized I was strapped into the mule's stokes frame.

My arm hurt.

"I gave you an injection," the mule said. "Emergency stimulant and glucose. Your vitals were dangerously low. You should eat something."

I undid the straps and sat up on the mule's back. Gray wet rock rose on three sides. A semi-circle of darkness loomed ahead.

The mule had brought me over the pass while I was unconscious. Ahead, the box canyon and the mine.

"He's in there," the mule said, helping me down from the litter. "He was determined to go. He's not the same."

"I tried to tell him. He wouldn't listen."

"Tell him what?" the mule asked.

"He made his choices before he ever left Texas," I explained. "He's a fool, but he comes by it honestly. I wouldn't have listened either. Here, help me walk."

A thousand meters down into the living granite, the tunnel widened into an enormous circular cavern.

We found him there. As I knew we would.

It was already too late. It had been too late for a long time.

Diego stood *changed* beneath the terrible light.

Cherubim stood like burning statues to one side, but it was the thing in the middle of the space that commanded our attention.

"I can *see* it," the machine said in wonder, awed. At long last it might have found the answers it was seeking. "What...is it? What *is* it?"

"It's you," Diego answered without turning. If he was surprised at the machine's curious self-awareness, he gave no sign. And showed no malice. "It's you in a million years."

It was a Throne.

Ancient text described them as great wheels with wheels covered in eyes, warriors, scholars, the Valiant One, the Seat and the Chariot of God.

And so, it was all of those things. And more.

It floated in the center of the huge space and filled the darkness with cascades of blinding light. Energy radiated outward in waves of furious heat that burned without consuming. Thunder crashed in a waterfall of sound without deafening and the still ground trembled with a power so vast it was beyond imagination.

And in the center of that dreadful maelstrom, *Genesis*.

The great beryl wheels of galaxies turned within galaxies, alive in the infinite heavens, their rims jeweled with a hundred billion suns like eyes. Fantastic star fields blazed with the glow of spilled milk beneath the crystalline vault, pulsing within a churning froth of dark matter and wild violet energy, shaped and twisted by gravity and time and vast unknowable forces. The universe, a thousand million universes, folded through each other, dimensions opened and closed like roses in boundless complexity beautiful and terrifying and a million years beyond human comprehension.

"It's a Gateway, I think. A door to Heaven. It's how *they* travel," I told the mule, nodding towards the Cherubim. "We're seeing only a single aspect of it, out of untold trillions. Can you feel it? It's a link to something far greater, something up there, raw intelligence, information, *purpose* and if that's not God, it might just as well be."

To look upon the Throne was to look upon the vast face of Creation itself across the endless width and unknowable depths of time. The Gods of human religion were small and petty in comparison, constructs of sticks and wire with glass buttons for eyes.

We stared into a place beyond understanding and our minds, man and machine, were altered in ways that could not be undone.

Diego dropped his carbine, forgotten. His pistol followed. He touched a control and his armor fell away to clatter on the stone. After a while, he turned to face me with two eyes clear and brown and terrible in their humanity.

There are indeed fates worse than mere death.

He had made his choice. And he would have to live with the consequences and, one day in the not too distant future, he would die with them.

And after that? I don't know.

He nodded to the Cherubim, a single human gesture of understanding. Shapes perhaps vaguely man-like and perhaps not turned within the light, something that might have been a head with a thousand shifting faces looked dispassionately back from the fire.

Diego placed a hand on my shoulder and left it there for a long moment, power flowed from his fingers.

Then he went to find his men.

✳✳✳

I know things.

And I wish that I did not.

I watched him walk away for the last time, down the trail away from the cabin. Six former soldiers, all that had survived, followed. He would find the rest of his companions on the long road back to Texas.

He said he had come to finish my mission, but it was never mine. Our destinies had not been our own for a very, very long time and this path had always been his to walk. His choice.

"We named him Diego," I said. "It once meant *teacher*."

I turned to go inside and prepare for the long trip home. I too would have a role to play one day. At the end.

The mule placed an actuator on my arm. I stopped and waited. After a while the machine said, "I think I now understand what you meant about faith without religion."

"I'm glad you found your answers."

"You're his mother," the mule told me, before it too turned to follow. "Be proud. He will be the greatest of all teachers. He will change the world."

"I know," I agreed sadly. "And they will crucify him for it."

Thirteen Things to Do Before the Apocalypse

Jane Yolen

1. Find a windowless room.
2. Put a vegetarian cookbook in your backpack.
3. Throw away your journal.
4. Study hypnotism.
5. Take up knitting.
6. Learn Chinese.
7. Buy extra guitar strings, eyeglasses, rope.
8. Find a complete Shakespeare.
9. Stock up on batteries.
10. Make cases of jam.
11. Gather in your children.
12. This time *really* love your neighbor.
13. Don't invest in futures.

After that, it's all downhill.

Alternative Apocalypse

The World of Bob

Rupert McTaggart Brackenbury

As dawn peeled back across the globe, one by one, Bob woke up.

As he woke, Bob realised something was profoundly wrong. The bed was too soft, the room too quiet. He was uncomfortably warm under a hill of blankets and threw them off as he leapt out of the bed. With rising panic, he understood that this wasn't his bed or his room and, more frightening still, he wasn't alone.

Another man was there, an imposing silhouette in the darkness.

Bob fumbled around the bedside table until he found a switch.

In the rosy bedside light, he could now see the other man was his exact double. This doppelganger was dressed in silk pyjamas too tight and too short. They looked like they belonged to an older woman. All but one of the buttons had popped. The doppelganger looked comical.

"I woke up," said Bob hesitantly. "I was here, it was too hot, I thought I should....."

"...Open the window?" Finished his doppelganger.

"You're me?"

"I think it's more like, *we're us.*"

Bob regarded what he was wearing; loose faux-satin boxers and a baggy t-shirt. He went to the nearest set of drawers, pulled out similar clothes, without questioning how he'd known where to find them, and handed them to his doppelganger. Doppelganger-Bob tried to find somewhere to change. Then, realising there was no modesty to be had, merely stripped off his too-small clothes, the last button on the silk pyjamas giving way as he did.

Bob cast around the room. It was luxurious, but with an oddly impersonal decor, as though none of it was designed to last. He looked at the photos on the nightstands, on the dressers, on the walls. He knew these people, not personally, just from the news.

"This is the Prime Minister's bedroom. *I'm* the Prime Minister."

"Yeah. Well, you were. Until just now."

"You're...you *were*...my wife."

"Yeah. I guess," Doppelganger-Bob replied, looking down at his new outfit.

The door opened cautiously and a familiar voice enquired awkwardly: "Um...Prime Minister? Sir? Can I come in?"

A third Bob, dressed in a too small suit, with a conspicuous earpiece dangling from his collar, entered the room.

The strangest thing was that none of them felt the least bit surprised.

❋❋❋

Every human on Earth was now Bob in mind and body. Whatever had caused the transformation took great care to cushion Bob's landing into his new lives. For some it was a hypnagogic jerk; a sudden sense of falling propelled Bob from sleep only to find himself in a stranger's place.

For other Bobs, it was like staring at a cupboard and realising he'd forgotten what he was looking for. He woke from an unconscious task to find he was driving to a home he'd never seen, or standing in an office he'd never worked in, suddenly aware of ill-fitting clothes or an uncomfortable chair.

The system wasn't perfect. Adjustment took a few seconds and for thousands of Bobs worldwide, those seconds proved deadly. For others, the sudden change in physical size or weight was dangerous, but most found the transition troublingly smooth.

Nearly eight billion Bobs, each an exact physical copy of the original, yet each Bob retaining the memories of the life he now occupied. The information was technical and dry, without fondness or regret, but whether he found himself performing surgery, flying a plane or parachuting out of one, every Bob knew what to do.

At least for now.

***

There'd been a terrifying noise a moment before, now it was gone, leaving a singing in Bob's ears and an echo of fear in his chest.

Bob got to his feet and looked around the gutted building he was standing in. He was short of breath, his heart beat fast, everything smelled of dust and smoke. He was wearing fatigues, a uniform he didn't recognise, his pack weighed heavily on his shoulders. Then in a wave he understood and was calm.

There'd been a tank. He looked for it and saw another version of himself stuck, one arm in and one arm out, of a hatch on the Tank's roof. The other Bob looked embarrassed as he tried to un-wedge himself. As Bob watched, he felt embarrassed too. He should have stuck to his diet better, done more exercise. But then who could have expected this?

Bob ran to help, clambering up the vehicle's side. Tank-Bob froze, not sure if he was in danger. Bob realized he still carried his rifle. He threw it to the ground—momentarily panicked it would discharge—and instantly relieved when it didn't.

"It's OK," Soldier-Bob said. "It's me. You. Whatever, I just want to help. Are you alone?"

From the muffled hatch, he heard another two Bobs inside. He put his arms around his double and pulled as the others pushed until Tank-Bob fell gracelessly out of the hatch. More Bobs arrived and together they helped free Tank-Bob's comrades.

Afterwards a dozen Bobs all stood by the tank, their number divided almost evenly into two uniforms.

"You were going to kill us," Soldier-Bob said rhetorically.

Tank-Bob looked ashamed. "Yeah but because you..."

Tank-Bob stopped. It was pointless. They all knew it was pointless. Not only was an argument going to be like playing chess against himself, it was to assign guilt for something he couldn't be responsible for.

"I think I'd like some breakfast," Tank-Bob said instead.

Soldier-Bob smiled. "Something light, you're going to need to squeeze back in that thing, it's blocking the road!"

The first thing every Bob wanted to know, once he'd got his bearings, was what had happened? Where was the original Bob? Bob Prime. He'd been quite content, hadn't he? Fairly anonymous, pretty average, maybe a little lonely, but he'd had a comfortable life.

"Maybe Bob, the real Bob, should be our king or something?" the Bobs asked themselves. They liked that idea. Bob wasn't keen on making decisions for other people, but now Bob would be making decisions for himself.

In a day or two, the whole world knew Bob Prime was dead.

The Doctor-Bobs were flummoxed. "We're an overweight 34-year-old male who doesn't get enough exercise, but that's not the cause of death. Maybe the process of copying him was fatal? Maybe you just can't make Bob more Bob?" one physician said to the Journalist-Bobs.

All the Bobs wanted to go to their own funeral but obviously, it wasn't practical. They put it on TV instead. The service was extremely short. Bob hadn't been religious, and no one wanted to eulogise themselves. There was talk about giving him a huge memorial or monument but that seemed vain. In the end, a large black gravestone was used, impressive but simple. All the Bobs felt good about that.

None of this resolved the question of what had happened. Scientist-Bobs and Philosopher-Bobs offered half-hearted suggestions. They even dragged the former Pope-Bob out of retirement on the slim chance he'd have some insight, but his guesses were even more unsatisfying.

No Bob could avoid the obvious: whatever had happened was plainly impossible and explaining it would require reassessing fundamental principles of what is and isn't reality.

Ultimately, all any Bob could do was get on with living.

Bob was surprised how much he enjoyed his new job.

He'd never thought of himself as tough or particularly macho but labouring seemed to be both those things. Prime Minister Bob had declared that for the time being every Bob would do the work of their former lives until they heard otherwise, but Bob had been unemployed and homeless so he was assigned a job and allowed to live in a motel.

Bob was happy; he'd been intensely anxious about the future. From what he could remember, the person he'd been before had felt the same way for much of their life.

"You're basically me," the motel owner had said. "I suppose we're closer than brothers."

Homeless-Bob had been so overwhelmed he threw his arms around Motel-Bob. Motel-Bob stiffened up, still unused to a world where everyone's intentions were transparent, but, realising it was innocent, he relaxed into it.

No-Longer-Homeless-Bob moved in next door to a pair of Bobs who had been a couple on holiday. They'd decided there was no point returning "home" to lives they had no feelings for and stayed on, though they moved into separate beds.

The supermarkets and shops had been generous as well. The Bobs who worked there gave him food and clothes for free. He wondered if this outpouring of generosity was just disguised self-interest, but Bob had never been political. He was just relieved, happy, happier than Bob Prime had ever been. He hugged the shopkeepers too. He hugged everyone he could. He became known as "huggy-Bob", and eventually just "Hug".

Word got around. "Hugs shouldn't die because of some fear of vulnerability or ingrained homophobia," he told the TV-Bob. "I don't know how this will play out, but," he stared down the camera," be kind to yourself, Bob. You're going through a weird time. You need a hug!"

Hug had started something important.

✳✳✳

Almost instantly, the world's economy started changing. Bob didn't need tampons or bras or contact lenses or allergy medication. He didn't want dolls or gold watches or fighter jets. There were billions of mass-produced items the world no longer needed or wanted, and so factories and businesses began to transform as well.

The first things they needed was shoes and clothes; fitting eight billion homogeneous Bobs into a world designed for variety in age, taste and gender was a monumental task. For the first few weeks, Bob wore whatever he could find that was comfortable. Things like dresses and skirts that Bob would have otherwise been embarrassed to wear were common. (There wasn't much embarrassment about anything anymore.)

As clothes and fabric were recycled, ugly multi-coloured or cheaply re-dyed boiler suits became the norm. Even when shortages ended, the relaxed style remained. The overalls and skirts, comfortable and practical, never quite went away.

Politics were transformed as well. In the first few weeks, the Politician-Bobs had all suggested elections, for the sake of fairness if nothing else. The other Bobs didn't see the point. "Who could represent me better than me?"

In the months and years that followed, Prime-Minister-Bob would often opine he had grown out of touch with the experience of everyday Bobs, but no one else wanted the job so Prime-Minister-Bob faithfully remained and did his best as the world wound down.

✳✳✳

Bob didn't care much for the report in front of him. The quality of the writing implied the Bob who'd written it hadn't cared much either. Around him were the Bobs who were now his best advisors.

"Can you summarise it for me? What's the bottom line? It's all bad news?" Bob had always been a glass half empty sort of guy.

"Not all Mr. Prime Minister..."

"*Please* call me Bob."

"Of course." The other Bob, a science advisor, took as little care with his appearance as he had with his report. He wore a loud shirt under a crumpled jacket. Behind him sat a small collection of useful Bobs, who'd inherited relevant knowledge and experiences.

The advisor talked quickly as if he had too many words to get out of his mouth before his turn was up. "Violent crime is at zero, crime in general is almost gone, and what's left are mostly mistakes and misunderstandings. Tax avoidance is way down, charitable giving is way up..."

"But there's no going back?"

"We don't know how this happened or why, so we can't reverse it, no. We looked at ways of bringing other people back. Cloning maybe? It's a process referred to as 'de-extinction' but it turns out that's not an option either."

"No women to carry the babies?"

"That is a problem, but we actually think we could work around it, if not with special incubators then with surrogates. Maybe chimps or gorillas?" He ignored the look on the Prime Minister's face. "No, the main problem is when we became Bob, our DNA became Bob's DNA. But it turns out so did all the other Human DNA: hair samples, discarded skin cells, unprocessed evidence kits, embryos prepared for IVF, dead bodies in morgues and cemeteries, even mummified remains in museums, they're all me, ah, I mean they're all *Bob*. In theory we could keep a long chain of Bob clones going indefinitely but..."

He trailed off, he didn't want to be the one to say it, so the Prime Minister did.

"...But no one want's that."

The silence was heavy.

Finally Science-Bob spoke up. "There's something else. It's mostly anecdotal, though."

"Go on. Please."

"We're seeing a lot of emotional detachment in the population. It might just be a normal response to trauma, or it could be another protection similar to the way we've retained the memories of the lives we took over. The worry is, we've always been pessimistic, and even the luckiest of us have been through something extraordinary. I'm, I mean, *we're* worried that this might be a sign that some of us aren't coping well."

"I've felt it myself, like inertia. It's hard to feel excitement about anything, but also hard to feel sad. We have a whole world struggling to find a reason to get out of bed."

"Can I make a suggestion?"

"Please."

"You've seen that story about the Bob they call 'Hug'?"

"Yeah."

"He's doing great work at a local level, reorganising his community to help out the Bobs who were left in difficulty by the transformation. I think we should apply that sort of thinking at every level, national, even global."

"I'm not sure, I mean, I don't want to do anything drastic then not be able to wind it back"

He noted the other Bobs in the room exchange glances. "Sir…"

"Bob."

"*Sir*," the advisor insisted "with all due respect, you're in an unprecedented position. Lots of people have had this kind of power but they never had the same insight to their citizens' needs or a real desire to help. I've spent a lot of time with these numbers. We're probably going to be the last generation, so if we want to achieve anything before we're gone, even if we just want to reduce suffering, then we need leadership. For better or worse, that's you."

The PM looked around the faces of the meeting. His face. Some of him looked annoyed, some worried, some exhausted, some terrified. He felt how lucky he had been to land where he was compared to some of his doubles. Since the transformation, changes had crept in but fundamentally, they were still the same person.

With a slight quiver to his voice he began. "I understand. I saw this Hug, on TV. He was saying we should be kind to ourselves, to each other, and I agree." He picked up steam as he spoke. His voice growing stronger. "I'll arrange a special session of Parliament and let everyone, the public included, know what you've told me. We need to ensure every Bob has a comfortable life, and if that means some of us need to make sacrifices, then so be it. It was all a lottery and I can't imagine I would object to helping out, especially not after hearing what some of me, some of *us*, are going through. I'll also contact my counterparts overseas, I'm sure they're reaching the same conclusions about now."

✳✳✳

Tastes changed dramatically.

Not only was the market for things Bob disliked effectively killed off, but once the bad news began to circulate, Bobs worldwide desired their food comforting and their entertainment distracting. Consumption of junk food soared. TV and movies became almost exclusively action films and comedies. Nothing new was being made, but there were enough things Bob had never got around to seeing to keep audiences happy. Books were similarly affected, except that tell-all confessionals in which Bobs revealed the secrets and experiences of their former lives regularly topped the best-sellers list.

Despite their emotional state, or perhaps because of it, the Bobs went about their new lives and responsibilities dutifully. They went where they were needed, helped as they were required, everyone shared, everyone took responsibility, no one alone and yet everyone the last man on earth.

Bob was lonely.

*** *** ***

Bob rubbed the pinprick on his neck and waited for the Doctor to tidy up. The chip was smaller than a grain of rice, but it was a comforting presence.

"Sore?"

"Mm-hmm."

"That'll pass soon. Do you mind me asking? Why'd you guys volunteer for this?"

Bob thought about those poor dogs, that girl at the high school, that woman at the bus stop. Fear swelled inside him. He answered in a small voice. "We all know who we were before. Not just Bob Prime, but who we were before we changed into a copy of him. That's why you get to keep being a doctor. Well I was..." He didn't want to say it aloud. "I did some bad things."

The doctor frowned. "It's strange. You're the first Bob I've met who doesn't think of himself as Bob Prime. The rest of us feel like we just woke up in the wrong place with some added memories to help out."

"The things I remember, even with the emotional detachment, I don't know that you can have them in your head and still be Bob."

"OK. I understand that I suppose. But why this?" He gestured to the needle before throwing it in a yellow plastic bin.

"I don't have the feelings or the desires, but I remember what it was like to have them. I know what it would feel like to do that stuff. It's scary to see who we could be if Bob's life had gone another way."

"That man's gone. He isn't who we are now."

"Not today. But no one knows what happened. I'm scared I'll turn back and do those things again. Or worse, I won't turn back and do those things again. They can't keep us in here forever but this way, if they ever need to track me down, that chip will help."

"In theory."

"Well, it's better than nothing, hopefully I won't ever hurt anyone else again."

"When do you get out of here?"

"Tomorrow. I got a job with a Bob they call 'Hug'. He runs a sort of charity to find work for people who aren't a good fit for the world, either this one or the one before."

Doctor-Bob put his hand out to shake. "Good luck, Bob. And you *are* Bob, no matter how you feel."

Bob smiled and grasped his hand. "Thanks. I Hope so."

✳✳✳

Population steadily shrank and by the time the Bobs were 44 almost a billion had died. The leading causes of death were now untethered from old age—instead disasters, accidents and infectious diseases claimed the most lives.

With the gene pool the smallest it had ever been, disease was more of a problem than ever. The Bobs who'd inherited the poorest parts of the world, those with less than ideal infrastructure, were decimated by an influenza pandemic before quarantines could be established and a vaccine deployed.

Globally, every Bob sacrificed as much as they could to help.

✳✳✳

Prime-Minister-Bob sat at the far end of the table chewing on his pen and waiting for the others to shuffle back from lunch. Each Bob wore a little flag sticker on their lapel with their country's name printed in large clear letters. Bob was never good with names or geography.

"Thanks guys, please sit. So, as we heard before lunch, globally we're now down to only 3 billion Bobs and that number is only going to continue shrinking."

"There's already too few of us to keep things running," one of the Pacific-Bobs interjected.

"Right, so here's the plan we've concocted: we choose, say, a hundred and fifty cities world-wide, places where the weather is mild and crops can grow, and we'll move every Bob to them. We'll consolidate our populations, and we begin to plan our…retirement."

Nervously, the Bobs all exchanged glances but none spoke.

Prime-Minister-Bob broke the silence "No one has any comments?"

Eventually one of the Scandinavian-Bobs replied. "It makes sense. It's not cheerful but it makes sense."

Prime-Minister-Bob let out a long sigh. "Honestly? I was actually hoping someone had another idea. Can we have a vote at least? All in agreement raise your hand."

The vote was unanimous.

✳✳✳

By the time the Bobs were 60, another four billion had died and most of the survivors had moved to retirement cities. The rest were safety-proofing a world to survive without human custodians.

Power plants had to be safely shut down. Toxic chemicals were disposed of as safely as the Bobs could manage. Dams and some larger buildings were dismantled. A lot of forests were planted.

Every zoo released its wards to their native habitats as best they could, animal crates circled the globe. Many of the beasts had never been free, but settled quickly into their now-empty ancestral homes. Some species were so endangered, only constant human intervention could stave off extinction; for those the Bobs could only make them comfortable.

Some animals, especially domesticated animals, simply had nowhere to go. There were too many lions in zoos for Africa to take all of them safely. Too many elephants for India. Too many kangaroos for Australia. Soon elephants and camels mingled with bison on the American plains.

In some parts of the world, feral dogs and cats could wipe out other species if they were just set loose. The emptying world was already overrun by rats, mice and cockroaches. The creatures that couldn't, or couldn't be allowed, to run free were culled. The exterminator-Bobs were busier than ever, a lot quit. Vegan food came back into fashion.

A few Bobs came up with the idea of a time capsule. It became a hugely popular endeavour for the remnants who busied themselves cramming as much human knowledge as they could into a container the size of a bus.

Choosing what to include was an emotional task. Ultimately, the capsule contained instructions for translation, a primer for 10 human languages and a warts-and-all history of the human species, its transformation into Bob and its retirement from the Earth. Any space that was left was filled with as much art and scientific knowledge they could cram in, either as a progress report or a leg up for whoever found it. Finally a Bob, recently deceased and preserved as best they could, was placed inside. It was both tomb and message in a bottle.

One hundred capsules were built. Ninety-nine were launched into space on robotic probes: to the Moon, Mars, other planets, other moons and in orbit around them. Half were sent out of the solar system on a slow crawl through infinity. Anywhere it was thought some future thing might have the thinnest of chances to find them.

The last was put inside a bunker in the dry valleys of Antarctica. The Bobs held a ceremony but in the end, even though it was televised, almost none of them watched.

✻✻✻

Bob sat watching the fire, lazily waving away the mosquitoes. His fish was cooking nicely, the low sun at his back, the air and sand were warm, waves lapped gently on the beach, he felt at peace.

He rubbed the scar on his neck, feeling the little implant under the skin. He'd once been worried about his previous life, but he'd lived far longer as another man.

Once Bob had heard a single voice calling out from across the globe. His own voice on phones and TV screens. But then satellites started switching off, and the world began to grow out of reach. They switched to radio but then, bit by bit, they failed too. It was unclear if it was the machines or the Bobs that had given up.

The last time he'd spoken to another Bob was two weeks ago. His own voice, thin and distant, an echo on the radio. The other Bob wasn't too far away, maybe a few hours' drive? That Bob had been a soldier, then a refugee, and finally another occupant of Hug's dormitories. They reminisced about the uncomfortable pillows and the excellent food. Eventually the other Bob had had to go. He had sounded so tired. Bob hadn't *seen* another living Bob for over a month.

Bob had been a horrible man before the transformation and a perfectly ordinary man afterwards. Now he was probably the only man there was.

Bob Prime had never thought highly of himself, quite the opposite, but in a strange way this Bob admired him. He'd never been intentionally rude. His desires had been mild as had his passions. He'd cared about others even if he was too shy to tell them. He'd given generously when he was able. He'd suffered a fair share of hardship and dealt with it as best he could.

It was the nature of Bob to have doubts, however. He may have been good and decent, but he'd never been ambitious. All they'd managed with command over the Earth was stewardship until retirement. Science, art, culture all stagnated. Even their transformation, an impossibility of physics and the greatest mystery of human history, had seemed too hard to pursue.

Bob would never know why he was chosen, but he felt confident it had been a good choice. For a few decades, all humanity had been united. No wars or racism or violence. Conflicts all settled reasonably. No one had taken too much or had too little. Everyone's sphere of concern encompassed everyone else. Even when he had retired, he'd done so gracefully, making sure to tidy up before he left. Thinking over it all, Bob allowed himself a sense of pride.

The fish was burning. Bob took it off the fire and laid it on a metal camping plate. He felt empty more than hungry. Maybe he'd feel like eating later. He lay down on his side, rolled his back to the fire, and closed his eyes against the last of the sun.

❋❋❋

Alone, as night folded over the globe, Bob fell asleep.

The Yes/No Machine

Stuart Hardy

REPORTER: It was approximately six months ago that the Republic of Libentia took the decision to replace its entire democratic process with a small plastic box that just says the words "yes" or "no" in response to any and all questions posed to it.

You join me now with senior civil servant Dominic Spokes.

So, Dominic: why exactly did the people decide to abandon their perfectly functional democracy in favour of adopting such a bizarre system?

CIVIL SERVANT: Well it's really very simple: you see, people had begun to feel that politics had become too complicated. Politicians would deliver long and boring speeches about trade, social care, international security and the like, but analysis showed that a staggering *ninety-seven percent of people* didn't understand a single thing they said. Two years ago, they elected President Greg Kinder, now the last President in our nation's history, who held the referendum on adopting his novel idea of completely binary and automated politics.

REPORTER: Right, so you just ask the machine a question, any question?

CIVIL SERVANT: Yes. It's passed legislation on everything from recycling collections to abortion rights. You simply ask it a question, and it just says yes or no. It's designed to be as simple as possible. You speak into this microphone here, and it will answer. Observe: MACHINE!

(There is a brief pause)

MACHINE: MACHINE IS LISTENING

(Civil servant picks up a card and reads)

CIVIL SERVANT: Machine, should we legalise the use of marijuana for medicinal purposes?

(There is a brief pause.)

MACHINE: YES

CIVIL SERVANT: There! See! That was very simple.

REPORTER: I see, I see. Does the machine explain how and why it comes to its conclusions?

CIVIL SERVANT: Well we did ask it if it would show us its working once, and it—

REPORTER: Said no?

CIVIL SERVANT: Well quite. The people don't really want the detail anyway. They don't care. They'll live with whatever they're given. They just want to have a system where they don't have to think about politics. That's the entire point of the Yes/No Machine: to make things simple and easy.

REPORTER: Does *anyone* know how it works and why? Surely the man who invented it knows?

CIVIL SERVANT: Well as it turned out, Professor Bartholomew was extremely depressed, and one day he ended up asking the machine whether or not he should kill himself, and it—

REPORTER: Said yes?

CIVIL SERVANT: Precisely. The machine's decisions are legally binding, so he *had* to do it; no backing out if he changed his mind.

REPORTER: I see. So I suppose my next question should be: how do you decide *what questions to ask it?*

CIVIL SERVANT: Well, the electorate send in their questions, and these questions are vetted beforehand so we know we're not gambling on something totally mad.

REPORTER: Right...and how do you vet the questions?

CIVIL SERVANT: Well, we ask the machine if we should ask it this question and it—

REPORTER: Says yes or no?

CIVIL SERVANT: Exactly! Pure and simple! No bias, no political partisanship, as fair as you could ask for. Though I will admit that I was a bit concerned when we had that question sent in asking whether we should exterminate all civilians under 30, but, well, we asked it and—

REPORTER: Oh, so that explains the death camps!

CIVIL SERVANT: Yes, quite.

REPORTER: And *that's* why you didn't send an ambassador to that UN summit last month about the concerns over human rights abuses in your country!

CIVIL SERVANT: Exactly! It said no! I'll admit I was concerned about the firing of our ambassador, but, well, the machine said yes, so we had to do it. I suppose it made sense once we'd started the death camps, you know: isolate ourselves from consequences on the world stage...I'm still not sure how the machine came to decide that saying yes to the death camps was a good idea in the first place, but still, the crime rate is greatly reduced.

REPORTER: But that's a bit of a barbaric policy, isn't it? Surely there should be some sort of system in place when considering extremist views?

CIVIL SERVANT: Well we would've implemented one, but the initial piece of legislation had nothing in it that defined what is and isn't an extremist view, everyone just sort of forgot about that, got caught up in the moment. It got passed by democratic means, so our hands are tied now, legally speaking. We did once put a question to the machine when someone came up with an amendment to the law regarding extremist questions, but—

REPORTER: It said no?

CIVIL SERVANT: Well, yes, quite. It's all a bit of a mess all told.

REPORTER: I suppose I'm lucky it said yes to grant me a work visa to come and film this interview.

CIVIL SERVANT: Yes, that was odd. I did wonder why it did that...

REPORTER: And you're sure the machine doesn't just answer at random? Are you sure it doesn't work like a magic eight ball? One day it could say yes to an idea, next day it says no? Ask again later? Are you sure it's not just a stupid lump of plastic?

CIVIL SERVANT: No, no, no, the machine *must* know what it's doing. The system *must* work! We haven't just put a magic eight ball in charge of our country, for God's sake!

REPORTER: Have you ever tried to open it up and look at its circuitry?

CIVIL SERVANT: No, we didn't do that because—

REPORTER: Someone asked it if they could open it up and look at its circuitry and it said no?

CIVIL SERVANT: ...how did you know that?

REPORTER: Lucky guess.

CIVIL SERVANT: Well yes, and we're bound by the machine now. The machine knows what's best.

REPORTER: But what if someone asks it something really quite dangerous, like: "Should we nuke North Korea?" for example?

CIVIL SERVANT: Ah, I'm glad you asked me that. You see, we have a safety procedure in place when it comes to international conflict. Just before finalising a tactical nuclear strike, a big box will pop up that says "ARE YOU SURE YOU WANT TO NUKE THIS COUNTRY? YES/NO?" and then we—

REPORTER: Ask the machine yes or no?

CIVIL SERVANT: Precisely!

REPORTER: I see.

Anyway, that's all for now. I'm certain that there'll be more eventually.
Back to you in the studio.

Alternative Apocalypse

Apocalypse

Ugonna-Ora Owoh

It came with cursing water,
hurting river, angry wind,
used to strike us down.
We were too unbearable.

Soldiers piled themselves into green-grey sacs
filled with concreted sands and bitumen stew.
Steeping their shaking guns
into the open-naked street.

Silence melted into our blood,
our heart raced with prayers,
the night made us ugly phoenixes in the dark.
And there it was,

like a mountain dressed with fire,
an indestructible demon,
we all thought,
abandoned the sharp in our voices and fled.

Soldiers firing bullet into empty ghosts,
street wounds flaming up.
And I looked behind
with piano-making music in my chest

and cried as the street
I called home burnt to ashes
in the dying dusk,

in the dying dusk without hope
and this became my own version of the book of
revelation.
The end time of flames,
my Apocalypse,
my Armageddon.

Alternative Apocalypse

The Janitor

Tomas Furby

Outside the storm raged, electric blue cracks across a black sky. Visibility was poor and detritus attacked the windows. A tin can man of buckled steel and rusted bolts trundled through the office muttering binary. The cleaning cart he pushed towered with every possible instrument of germ carnage. There were mops and dusters and clear plastic bottles filled with liquids so corrosive their labels had long since faded to white.

Emergency lights glowed green over dark exits. Air conditioning hissed and crackled at him from above. He jangled back at it, humming a tune of ones and zeros that sounded a little like David Bowie's "Ashes to Ashes". He took a duster from the cart and wiped a thin white layer from the nearest desk. Two squirts of polish, one jerky circle forwards, one backwards. Wax on, wax off, he whispered, and chuckled a theremin.

He moved from desk to desk as he did every day. Top left to bottom right; two squirts with the polish; wax on, wax off. He was a pro. Best cleaner FedEx had ever seen. They'd given him a trophy at the 2030 Staff Awards. Wheeled him out of the basement specially. He didn't have any protocols for award ceremonies, so sat quietly in the corner until they asked him to take the stage. He said thank you when the boss shook his hand and everyone clapped. It was a good day. The trophy sat on the top shelf in his closet, proudly displayed, polished twice a day until the enamel wore off. Employee of the year.

The sun rose, sliding light across the room. The storm was dying. Dust streaks across windows turned gold. It was going to be a lovely day. Perhaps everyone would make it to work after all. The robot, who liked to be called Wilson the

Janitor by his colleagues because he thought it was rather grand to have a capitalized name and a title, stopped and performed the robotic equivalent of a frown—which is to say, he went quite still and trained his little red sensors on the large rusty stain on the carpet for a few seconds. He had no expression as such but he tried very hard for quizzical. "Oh dear," he said, "someone's spilt their tea again."

Wilson turned grinding gears to the cart. Something inside him crackled and sparked. One arm rose and hovered over the selection of bottles. It got caught in invalid memory and twitched a few times until he slapped it with his other arm and it rebooted. The steel echo rang through the office. "Getting old," he muttered, and groaned. He was definitely due a service. Perhaps it was time for another memo to IT. They hadn't been down to see him in ages. He picked a bottle with a particularly viscous green liquid inside and bent to scrub at the carpet. Red stained his sponge. Not tea then. More like tomato juice, or wine. Maybe the execs partied a little too hard with clients last night. He scrubbed harder, refusing defeat. Time passed, he wasn't sure how much. The light had moved when he stood. The carpet was no longer red. It was worn and fibrous in a patch, a little floorboard showing through. Wilson trundled toward the kitchen, singing the song that dial-up internet made in the nineties.

He'd worked at the office for a long time. Unsure how long. His hard drive was full and no one had defragged him for a while, so he no longer recorded every day. There was no need really; he had just enough RAM available to perform within the parameters of his role indefinitely if he didn't fill up on useless information.

There were a few early birds sitting at their desks, tucked into their ergonomic chairs, all silently staring at screens. The computers booted up automatically at 7:30, filling the room with the hum of steel fans and loose wires. Wilson waved genially as he went past. They didn't move. One made a crumbling sound and slumped forward. Wilson tutted to himself. "Heavy night was it, Delia?" Delia didn't answer. Wilson shrugged. Delia was an alcoholic. The wind outside howled particularly hard and somewhere upstairs a door slammed. The sound of broken glass falling. Wilson sighed.

More work. Couldn't people close doors gently? Why all the slamming? He added it to the list. He'd send a polite reminder round later.

The kitchen was dark. Wilson flipped the switch and light bars flickered. One was dim and sputtering. The other couldn't decide whether 'on' was a function it performed anymore and made mournful buzzing sounds of indecision. A shadow sat in one corner. "Is that you, Chuck?" Wilson squinted into the dark, or would have had he eyes. He quite liked the idea of squinting. He tried it again. Maybe if he cut the light to pixels 5 through 102 so his sensors turned into little red bars...he raised one hand in salute over his makeshift squint like a sailor perusing the horizon. Chuck was slumped at one of the green plastic tables nursing a cup of cold tea and didn't seem to appreciate the squint as much as Wilson would like.

"Morning, buddy!" He creaked over to the sink and began running the hot tap. A few flakes of rust crumbled off and scattered a breadcrumb trail across the sticky kitchen lino. "Crazy storm we had this morning, eh? I nearly didn't make it in."

He waited for Chuck to laugh at that—everyone knew Wilson lived in the basement—but Chuck wasn't breathing. Wilson sighed static. Must've been a rough night. He was looking slightly more desiccated than usual. Chuck had a newborn, wasn't getting much sleep. Nice guy though, appreciated a joke, never snapped. Always took the time to hang out in the kitchen, have a chat. Not everyone liked bots for some reason, but Chuck was one of the good 'uns.

Perhaps now was the opportune time to practice his new trick. Wilson grinned, or would have had he a mouth. He turned from the sink, leaving the tap running because the boiler was taking its time again, and rummaged in the cart. A robot rummaging can be quite chaotic. Bottles and rags spilt from the cart in an avalanche. He didn't notice. "Hey Chuck, watch this." Chuck watched.

From the rubble Wilson reverently raised a small black tube. He'd found it on the side next to the dryer in the women's loos. It was almost new. He'd posted a note on the bulletin board in Lost and Found but nobody replied, so it was his now. As he twisted it, a crimson bullet revolved out. Slowly, shakily, he raised it to his slate-grey globe head. He'd only done this once, in his cleaning closet after hours, and he'd had a mirror then. It might go horribly wrong, but Chuck looked like he could use a laugh.

Wilson painted a smile on what passed for his face. It was a wider curve than anyone human could grin and a little lopsided, but generally pretty friendly looking. He finished it off with fake dimples at each end which made it look a little less like Pat Bateman laughing over business cards.

"What do you think, Chuck?"

Chuck's head fell backwards in a cloud of dust, his mouth gaping open in silent laughter. Wilson burbled static happily to himself. Perfect. He turned back to the sink. The water was still cold. Boiler must be broken. He turned off the tap and stared remorsefully at the dusty mugs stacked on the sideboard. He'd have to email Facilities. He didn't like Facilities. They always had an automatic reply on saying they'd get back to him and never did. Slumping a little, internally he composed the note:

✳✳✳

Dear Richard,

I hope you are well. Please note it appears the boiler is no longer functioning. Ran the hot water tap in the kitchen for 3.17 minutes this morning and sensors indicated temperature of 5 degrees. Please can you take a look as I have been unable to wash up today. Thanks for your help.

All the best,

Wilson the Janitor :)

✳✳✳

He cc'd his boss, Mr. Zemeckis, just in case anyone complained about the dirty crockery, and hit send. Nothing happened. He hit send again. Nothing happened. An error message tickled the back of his head with warning lights. No signal. "Searching...please move closer to router." Well wasn't that just a bug in the code. The whole office would be up in arms if the internet was down. How was anyone supposed to get any work done? Ever since they downsized

IT and outsourced to India, service had been particularly poor.

Well, if he couldn't do the dishes then that was this floor done. He checked his clock. It was showing an improbable date, around 11:15. He was definitely in need of a tune up. Soon as the Wi-Fi was back he'd email Mandeep about penciling something in. Chuck's head was still thrown back, either laughing or asleep, so Wilson just waved and said "See ya later, Chuck. Stay frosty." He wasn't entirely sure what the saying meant, but the delivery guy with the long hair and the legalize marijuana t-shirt had said it to him once and he rather liked the expression. "Stay frosty, Chuck." Wilson pressed the light switch as he left and the flickering room plunged into darkness.

The windows down the corridor were thick with grime. Bloody light drifted in beams through the dusty dark wherever dirt didn't smear glass. Wilson bobbed his head slowly side-to-side, like a volleyball drifting into the ocean, lost. He'd have to put in a requisition order with Facilities as well. He made a note to get onto them tomorrow. Those windows were truly disgusting. It looked like they hadn't been cleaned in years. In decades. What was longer than a decade? The cart rattled along in front of him, echoing through the building. He called the elevator. Something dark smeared the blue ring round the call button like a slashed zero. Wilson cleaned it while he waited. Slowly, deep down in the bowels of the building, the lift rumbled upwards like Lucifer rising for breakfast.

Floor by floor, Wilson the Janitor worked his way through the building, dusting desks and cleaning kitchens and sweeping broken glass. Top left to bottom right, kitchen, bathroom, lift; top left to bottom right, kitchen, bathroom, lift; top left to bottom right, kitchen, bathroom, lift. A few colleagues noticed his new smile and replied with their own: toothy and wide and a bit boney. One guy was so tickled he fell out of his chair and didn't get up. The bathroom on 5 was flooded. The lift wouldn't go to 19. A bar light hung from the shadow of broken ceiling panels and wires on 32, dust trickling down, humming gently. It was all a shambles, not like the old days at all. They used to run a tight ship at

FedEx. It had gone to the dogs since the new CEO came in. The company was operating a skeleton staff and the building was falling apart.

He made the top floor around 3:30. It was empty, quiet, and there was definitely more broken glass than usual. Air whispered through shattered panes like ghosts swirling cirrus dust. Wilson's tracks crackled over frost. "Brrrr," Wilson said, staring down at the cluttered street. There'd been a pileup below. Scattered cars abandoned like a toddler's toy set. "I hope no one was hurt," he whispered, clutching his rag. A few flakes of snow drifted onto his head from boiling black clouds in an apocalypse sky. They melted and trickled tears down his sensors.

Wilson's internal clock flashed 4pm. Home time. He was quiet now, buzzing gently. His sensors flickered like that last bar on a phone's battery. He checked diagnostics. Just enough juice to make it home. Switched to low power mode just in case. Wouldn't do to shut down in the middle of a corridor. Someone would have to come and wheel him back down to the basement. Maybe Chuck would do it. He liked Chuck.

His electric shuffle was slower on the return journey. The lift waited for him at the end of the corridor like an old friend ready for after-work beers. He smiled and patted it on the side as it delivered him to BF. "Same time tomorrow, Lenny?" The lift dinged and closed its doors.

Wilson rolled his cart into the cleaner's closet and sidled over to the charge port. His colleague Betty was plugged in already, powered down. Her arm was raised slightly, clenched hand at a right angle towards him. He fist-bumped her gently as he buzzed past, too tired to talk. Betty's eyes were dark and her charger cracked and sparking.

Wilson the Janitor leant back in his charging dock and propped his tracks up on the cart, switching to charging mode. It had been a long day. Hopefully the Wi-Fi would come back soon. There were a lot of memos to send. 372 on the list. Honestly, the state of the place. You'd think the end of days had come or something. A system message scrawled neon words across his display as the charger powered up.

Low disk space: you are running out of disk space on Local Disk (C:). To free up space on this drive by deleting old or unnecessary files, please reply affirmative.

Wilson nodded once, slowly, and deleted the day.

Outside the storm raged.

Alternative Apocalypse

The Vision

Melvin Sims

The Reverend General Barry Fallbad Junior was sitting on the edge of his pool when the alerts came out.

He didn't pay any particular attention. He was focused. His daiquiri was fresh, the pool boy was working his oiled body diligently to skim the pool, and another was busily arranging the deck chairs in preparation for the celebration.

And what a celebration it would be.

It was the five-year anniversary party of approval of the Faith-Based Missile Defense System. The brainchild of the Reverend Barry Fallbad Senior, God rest his soul. Now seven years gone, as was the prostitute in whose arms he had died. There were some things best kept in the family.

He smiled to himself at the memory.

The deep blue of the pool almost glowed in the morning light; the golden tiles that lined its sides were particularly beautiful this time of day. He couldn't look at them without thinking of the many millions of people who made up the Faith-Based Missile Defense system, praying in shifts around the clock, offering supplication to the Lord Jesus himself to place the power of God between the United States and the heathens whose missiles threatened these God-fearing lands with nuclear destruction.

Of course, he also thought of the billions, many billions, the defense department paid him to keep it in place. He wondered vaguely if platinum would work in the jacuzzi.

The scientists, those fools, had claimed it would cost trillions to build a system capable of stopping the Indian, Chinese, Pakistani, Russian, French and Korean missiles.

Then came the Vision, the Great Vision. He revealed it Live on Sunday morning TV, with just a bit of help from the Fallbad Ministries graphics department. It was magnificent.

A Vision of the Sword of Michael striking the missiles from the sky where they would fall uselessly into the North Arctic Sea.

Junior had thought pleasantly at the time that the giant blond-haired Michael of his vision had looked a bit Chris Hemsworth, but the point was made to the faithful.

Congress had objected at first. But the Fallbad Ministries war chests were full, the people inspired, and the opposition quickly collapsed.

The results were stunning, 24 hours a day, prayers were streamed from the padded altars of the country tabernacles, chapels, wherever the faithful gathered and prayed against the missiles.

And now? Now he was contemplating a platinum Jacuzzi. He sipped his daiquiri and marveled at the greatness of it all.

When his cell phone began to ring more urgently, he gave it a glance. He recognized the number. The President. Probably calling to say he'd be late.

He never got the phone to his ear.

He never heard the whine of the missile.

He never saw the pool vaporize, the gold tiles melt. The shadow of the pool boy burned into the wall by the flash. If he had, he might also have noticed the giant figure in the sky wielding a flaming sword, a figure that looked absolutely nothing like Christopher Hemsworth.

Punxsutawney Eulogy

Patrick Winters

His black containment suit stood out stark against the all-encompassing white and gray of the forest about him. Specks of white swirled through the chilly air, whipping and wafting against the thick outer padding of the Level A gear; still, he could feel the cold seeping through the protective layers. He shivered as he huffed his way through shin-thick drifts of white, his thick boots awkward to trek in, his breather working overtime in the closed hood, and his gloved hands grasping his rifle with determination.

This wintery wonderland was made of ash, not snow. The ash of the world. And the only real "wonder" to it was wondering how long one could survive out in its barren and silent miles.

Now, in the frigid desolation of it all, he didn't wonder anything of the sort. Survival had gone from being an essential, to a commodity, to a non-issue. Revenge—or whatever he could muster of the notion—had taken its place. He stopped and scanned the land, peering through the ghostly trees. They swayed like mournful pallbearers carrying off a dead, gray sky on their charred and withered shoulders. They were skeletons of themselves, their leaves and color long gone, replaced with thin black trunks and branches that rose weakly towards the bleak heavens. He gazed at the ground about their bases, looking for any tracks leading through the mounds of ash that caked the spoiled earth. He saw none. He kept on anyway.

His wife was dead. Had been for a week now. He'd buried her within the walls of their underground bunker, laying her to so-called rest next to their son. The child had died the week before that. Both had fallen ill—too direly ill for his paltry stash of medical supplies to do anything for. He had known—those twenty years ago, when he started putting his wealth and time into constructing the bunker—that illness would be the wild-card he could never properly account for, should the worst occur. And by the time the worst *did* occur, he had managed to sufficiently guard and prepare the bunker—along with its generators, storage areas, and air filtration system—and he had stock-piled tons of food and supplies to last them for a long, long time beneath the earth. But still, the potential for illness—and the few capabilities at hand to treat more serious instances—had loomed over his head. And a long time of living under a ruined world could bring many chances for something to go wrong.

Two years had passed since the sirens sounded and every nation's sky filled with arches of fire and smoke, and the family of three had managed to get by, waiting for the day when they could have the ground beneath their feet again instead of all around them. To feel a welcoming breeze against bare skin. To know the nurturing warmth of the sun. To live like a free person, rather than a cowering rodent within lead-laced walls. But once their boy had begun coughing up blood, he knew their so-called luck had run out; no number of medications or manuals could help him save his son. He needed a physician and a hospital, and those didn't exist anymore. And when his wife started to spit up scarlet as well, he knew he had failed his family.

His boy died, and his wife gave in to the same ailment—though she was helped along by a broken heart. He had been left alone and hopeless, numbed by his failure to save his family from the inequities of a world gone wrong. He stewed in the silence of the bunker for a while, wondering if a bullet or a length of rope would work better to end his sorrows. But then the rage set in, and the idea of revenge took root. Not long after that, he had hefted his containment suit on (not because he was afraid of dying in the still-bad air above ground, but because he was afraid of dying *too soon* in it) and grabbed his Springfield M1A Loaded .308 rifle off its rack. With an extra magazine of ammo and nothing else, he'd stepped into the shelter's elevator and taken it up, climbing the half-mile between the bunker and the surface. When he stepped out of it and into the wilderness, he had no real thought of ever returning.

Now, with the bunker a near mile to his back, he entered into another dense copse of dead trees, keeping his eyes peeled. He stopped again and looked about, trying to decide if he should maintain a straight shot into the forest or take a turn this way or that. He elected to make a slight adjustment eastwards, hoping that the elusive figure of his vengeance could be found that way.

As he turned, he stumbled over a rock that lay hidden beneath the ash, his steel-toed boot thumping against the protrusion and jarring him. He pitched forward, losing his balance and falling to his hands and knees. The stock of his rifle smacked against the ground, and the hood around his head crinkled and rustled against his ears, adding to the pressures bearing down upon his aching head. He sighed ragged breaths into his breather as he knelt there a moment. Then, grabbing hold of his rifle, he stood up and charged on into the forest with an enraged yell. He ran through nothing, towards nothing, away from nothing. Nothing remained save for a single, small chance to gain some twisted and insane sense of vindication.

His son had been too young to understand what had happened to the world, back when the words and yelling of politicians ceased and the rumble of explosions took their place. When he and his wife had rushed him off to their secret shelter, clearly the boy had been terrified, but hadn't questioned matters. And when the boy did finally ask why they couldn't go back up above ground and return home, he didn't have the heart to explain the true situation to his son. So, bumbling for some sort of answer, he'd said that the groundhog had seen its shadow and there'd be six more weeks of winter, like the old tradition said—and what a bad winter it would be. A nuclear winter, as a matter of fact. His wife had not appreciated the poor excuse of an explanation, but she hadn't ever found the words to tell their son the truth of things, either.

How could you help a youth understand what you—with all your years and knowledge—couldn't rightly understand, either? When the first six weeks were up, their son asked if they could go up again; they'd said no. Their son asked why. And he had told him. "It's still winter—that groundhog must have had one *big* shadow." And so it went, on and on, and their young boy grew to loathe and wail over the mean groundhog that kept his family in the dingy bunker for so long.

"I hate that groundhog, daddy," he heard his son crying from the past. "I hate it!"

"I do, too, bud," he said now, as he had said to his boy back then. He gripped his rifle tighter, his finger millimeters away from the trigger and itching to close the distance.

His limbs screamed from exertion and he started growing dizzy, maybe from lack of oxygen, maybe from sheer delirium—he didn't really know or care which it was. As his head spun and his throat grew raw from hollering, he lost his balance again and careened straight into a blackened hemlock. He fell to his side, barely keeping a grip on the rifle. The tree creaked and rocked precariously, then came tumbling down with a harsh crack in its trunk, landing inches from where he lay. He was pelted with its branches, the thin limbs snapping off and breaking across him with just enough force to wrench a pained growl out of him. He rolled over and away from the felled tree, cursing all that was left to be cursed.

He got to his knees and crawled along a short ways, head held low as he started to cry, the tears slipping off his haggard cheeks and dripping down onto the plastic covering of his hood. Drip, drip. When he looked up and ahead, he saw the snarling face of a wolf lunging straight for his own, teeth bared and hot breath fogging up the front of his hood.

He fell onto his back with a shout, the wolf missing his face and grabbing hold of his arm instead. He felt its teeth dig into his suit, their tips brushing against his skin. The beast shook its head ferociously, trying to either tear his limb off or drag him away. The teeth now tore his skin, drawing blood and pain. Reacting in terror, he brought the forearm of his rifle down, once, twice—three quick times across the back of its skull, roaring like a berserker in the midst of ancient battle. The wolf yelped and drew back, stains of red now soaking the top of its crud-covered head, and he brought the tip of the barrel up and towards its side as he rolled back onto his knees.

He pulled off a hurried shot right as another wolf came rushing up and launched itself at his side with a ferocious growl. Its face smacked against his, and man and animal fell in a pile. The wolf arched its deformed head this way and that as they rolled about, biting at his hood and tearing it away piece by piece. He felt the chill of the day strike him in the face like an icy punch. He smelled the animal's decaying, dirty scent through his breather. And he saw its tumor-spotted snout pull the last of the plastic face-cover off before he found his strength again, driving an elbow up into the animal's gut.

He hauled it off of him, tossing it up as it did a somersault into a drift of ash. He rose up to his feet as it started to do the same, and clutching his rifle in both hands, he put three rapid shots into its side. It howled as red spurted out from its balding coat of fur, dead by the time the third bullet tore out through its flank. No sooner had it fallen still than its compatriot—the first wolf, limping along from its wound, but still alive—latched its jaws down onto his left leg. Groaning through gritted teeth as the wolf's fangs tore at his pants, flesh, and tendons, he shoved the barrel of the gun square against the animal's brow. He squeezed off another shot, the sound of the canine's skull cracking mixing with the roar of the gunfire. Its bite loosened as it died, but still, he emptied the magazine into its back, shouting out his own howls until the blaring shots turned to weak clicks of the trigger.

He pulled the gun away and wobbled a few small steps from the canine's corpse. He pulled off the remains of his breather, now useless and torn from the surprise assault. Then he threw up the paltry contents of his stomach, his nausea rising from a combination of the still-flowing adrenaline in his veins, the fetid smell of the dead wolves, and the thick, tainted air that clawed its way down his throat. Shaking and struggling to breathe, he stumbled further away from his kills. He ejected the spent magazine from his rifle as he hobbled along, pulling the spare from his belt and smacking it with unsteady hands into the rifle. He gagged, then coughed, feeling his wounds bleeding and burning beneath his compromised suit. Too late to do anything about it now; too careless to do anything, either— so he kept on with his search, limping along as the falling flecks of ash started to coat his face and hair.

A few dozen steps brought him up to a small hole dug into the side of a gently-rising, soot-smothered hill. He looked down into it and saw three wolf pups peeking out at him. They were small, perhaps a few months old, rail-thin and frail, completely hairless, and whimpering softly as they stared out to the trees. They looked to him, heads hung low, and then back out to the trees. One of them gave a feeble bark with its snub snout, its call going unanswered. He swallowed down the nasty taste of bile and sick in his mouth before firing multiple shots into the den. The whimpering stopped and he went on his way.

Time passed—how much, he couldn't say. Seconds, minutes, hours—it didn't matter. What use was time when, for all you knew, you were the only one alive to count it? The sky above remained the same dull gray all the while, neither darkness nor sunlight taking it for their own. The freezing winds continued to stir, numbing his cheeks as they turned pink—from the cold, red burn on his skin and the white frost and ash that gradually came to rest over it. Soon his bitten leg went numb, and he was forced to drag it along behind him. He used the rifle as a crutch when a fair slope rose up along his path; he ascended it with sluggish, taxing effort— so much so that he collapsed the moment he cleared it, the land smoothing out again to stretching, endless woods ahead.

He crawled on his belly over to another charred hemlock, breathing in the ash that surrounded him. He hacked and spat it out when flurries of the stuff found their way onto his tongue. When he reached the tree, he sat up and leaned against it; it creaked some, but stayed up strong against his weight. He straddled the rifle between his knees and set his chin down to his heaving chest, shutting his eyes, his body longing for rest more than his still-wild and angry soul. But now, after the wolves and the ruining of his suit, his desperate search seemed all the more foolhardy and impossible, and it was only a matter of that pointless time until he died out here.

He leaned his head back against the hemlock, staring up into the gray sky as his thoughts swirled. He wondered if even God had been burned off His throne way up there, the fires that scorched the earth those two years ago taking any semblance of Paradise with them. Down here, amidst the ruin, the idea seemed terribly plausible. Or maybe He had gone long, long before that—and that was why this had all been allowed to happen to the world. The idea only pushed him further into the arms of madness, and he let it hold him.

The sound of something moving through the ash came from a few feet away. He turned his head and eyes to the direction of the subtle disturbance, gripping the rifle and drawing it closer to him. A short ways off to his left, a patch of ash was rising up from the rest of the undisturbed layers about it. It cracked and crumbled like an anthill as something crawled up from the ground below. A small, brown head poked through the stuff, shaking it off of its dirty fur. It looked this way and that as its stubby body rose on its hind legs, standing proud, with its little forelegs close to its chest. The creature turned and looked his way, taking him in with one eye (the other was hidden beneath a nasty growth on its head) and with its little front teeth jutting out of its whiskered mouth.

He gazed at it, and it gazed at him. Then, breaking from his amazement and his stunning sense of triumph, he hauled up his rifle and fired. The animal—a good-sized groundhog—exploded into furry bits and strings of bloody flesh as he screamed out his teary cheers of revenge. A bloody hole in the ash was all that remained of the thing, and it made him laugh and wail all the more. He kicked his legs and pumped his arms, calling out to all of the dead world, to his wife, but more so, to his son, hoping they all could hear.

"I got the fucker!" he shouted, laughed, and cried out all at once. "I got him! I got him! I got him..."

His back slipped off of the tree and he shoved the rifle aside. He lay down on his side, sticking his head into a pile of ash and not caring in the least about it. He pulled his legs up to his chest and set his arms over his head as he continued to mumble, "I got him...I got him...I got him..."

More chilling winds picked up, gaining greater force and sending flurries of soot over him. It covered him in a matter of moments, and if anyone had been around to see it, they would have heard the faint murmur of his voice saying "I got him" coming up from the ash long after he had disappeared beneath it.

Living in the Gleam of an Unsheathed Sword

Andrew Davie

The Wall

It was a rubble stone wall measuring fifteen feet high and stretching across the horizon. At night, aching and spent from his labor, Spero lay on his dirty mattress, plagued by nightmares of unseen forces dismantling the day's efforts erecting the wall. He'd forgotten how long he'd been indentured. Spero could only guess his age; somewhere between twenty-five and thirty-five. His knowledge of how to assemble the wall had been second nature to him, but it was still daunting. Even with an entire crew, the job would take a lifetime. Alone, he was weighed down by the incomprehensible vastness of the endeavor.

When he asked, he was told the wall cordoned off the owner's property. How far did the property line extend? Farther then you can see. Was there a quarry nearby? More questions were usually met with violence.

Tools and materials had always been there when he awoke. Once he cleared five feet, it was necessary to use the scaffolding, and a counterweight pulley system, which could be wheeled as he moved further down.

The physical taxation took its toll in the beginning but now only plagued him during times of sickness. The mental fatigue broke him repeatedly, and he would flail about at night. Long ago, he stopped directing his ire at the owners. He'd never met them, wasn't even sure they existed, save for hearsay and conjecture. Spero kept his focus on work and bided his time.

Andrew Davie

Furman

The Overseer had a sawed-off shotgun with him at all times. He sat in a fold-out chair adjacent to a red and white cooler full of beer. Spero never saw him eat. A beach umbrella jutted out of the ground next to him. Every so often, he'd play a dinged-up boom box which only got a classic rock station half of the time. He was permanently red by the sun and the drink. Blonde hair, almost white, in a crew cut, wraparound sunglasses, and an enormous gut. Hairy, unconscionably hairy. He wore a brace on his left leg. By eleven in the morning, he'd already be drunk, but he would never pass out or get sick. The Overseer lived in a trailer, only thirty feet away from Spero's. Both rickety old Jetstreams moved in conjunction with the wall's growth. Otherwise, the land was sprawling green immensity.

The first few times Spero attempted to mutiny, The Overseer shed his haze and beat Spero senseless. Underneath the doughy frame, The Overseer was carved from granite. Though crippled, he still moved swiftly. Spero had long since given up on a direct attack.

Spero fit another stone to the random courses, pinning it in place with the mortar and smaller stones set in the joints. The sound of scraping occasionally muted by the wind.

"I always feel like somebody's watching me." The Overseer echoed Michael Jackson's voice until static disrupted the song from the boom box.

The Overseer's name was Furman, but Spero preferred to keep him nameless. It would make it easier on the day he finally got his revenge.

"Just keep thinking about the next stone," Furman said as if he could read Spero's mind.

His fingers long since calloused over and deformed, Spero gripped the dense rock and lifted it onto the newly formed row. Wiping the sweat from his brow, he positioned it to fit snug amongst its brethren.

"I work from nine to five, hey Hell, I pay the price," proclaimed the tinny speakers.

The Overseer produced another beer from his cooler and popped the top. Foam spilled on his stained tank top. Spero picked up another rock. Sometimes, after being pushed too far, he would throw his rock at Furman. Most of the time, he missed. One time Furman shot the stone into fragments. Another time it connected. Spero was laid out for a week after that reprisal.

He'd spend hours, days, contemplating the correlations of size and weight of the perfect stone which would achieve the greatest velocity while maintaining enough force to do any permanent damage. But the opportunity rarely presented itself. Furman always kept his distance and the shotgun pointed. Always one step ahead, warning Spero to keep his mind on work just around the time thoughts of revenge began to manifest. One day, though, he would find a suitable weapon and his wrath would be satiated. Until then, he'd have to stomach arduous work and horrible renditions of '80s songs.

Spero

He'd have the same dreams each night: memories of a man taking care of him; possibly his father. He had no memories of his mother. There was only the man whose face was blurry but exuded kindness. There was a strength about this man. Youth. Vigor. His father had been working on the wall. Spero watched until he got old enough, then began to help. Eventually, the memories ceased and a blank spot occupied the timeline until Spero was fully grown. Dim recollections of a third man and an altercation. He could sense a violent trauma responsible for the lost period of memory.

At the end of the day, when he returned to his trailer, he'd have a cupboard stocked with canned goods. He never saw anyone come or go. After cooking a meal on his hotplate, he'd retire to his mattress and read; something else he must have picked up from his father, but like masonry, never remembered doing so.

Occasionally, he'd have a vivid dream in which he killed Furman. Except it wasn't him or Furman but men who resembled them. Hands would finally wrap around a large enough stone which would hurl toward the captor. The accompanying sound would always change depending on the trajectory. Sometimes it would be two pieces of wood clapping together, and other times the biting of a fresh apple. Scrambling, picking up the stone, and bashing, but Spero always awoke before the final blow.

The following morning, the whole process would begin again. It would continue for the rest of his life, or until he'd paid his debt.

The Owners

When he was younger, Furman would allow more questions.

"Who are the owners?"

Furman turned down the volume on the boom box. He craned his neck toward an unseen domicile, and when he faced Spero, had a forlorn look on his face.

"Generations owned this land. Wealth like you couldn't believe."

"Pay you much?"

Furman laughed, cracked another beer.

"You just keep working, and maybe you get out of here while you can still walk."

Spero never saw anyone except for Furman. Yet, everything would always appear out of thin air. Sometimes, Spero would see mirages of cars driving toward them through the vast dirt and brush. Salvation. He was never given a straight answer to how much of the wall needed to be completed for him to "Settle his account." Furman would be enraged once the topic switched to debt.

One day, fed up, Spero asked: "What if I stop working?"

Furman picked up the shotgun and laid it across his knees.

"You stop working on this wall, it means you've ceased paying back your debt. The only way any of us stay alive is if we do our jobs and that wall gets built."

Mary

Long ago, toward the beginning of his servitude, Furman said there would be rewards. Positive re-enforcement so to speak. He was given books. A voracious reader and autodidact, soon Spero developed his theoretical understanding of things. Ultimately, Mary, too, was added.

Having no practical application of his knowledge, he was awkward in every sense of the word, uncertain of how to act on instinct. The concept of love and sex had never been addressed, and though he could feel an overwhelming desire, he was reticent. She was older, already seasoned. Spero asked questions incessantly. She silenced him. Their lovemaking was one-sided but cleansed him of anxiety and rage. In the aftermath, he put his arm around her but felt no warmth.

"Why?" he asked once.

"We're all working off one debt or another," she finally said in the darkness.

They rarely spoke after that. Spero surmised that like him she must live nearby. Perhaps there was a whole commune of serfs like him spread out over the vast empire and keeping them separate prevented a possible revolution.

Once a month, Mary would come to visit, a relic of a once beautiful person. At night, she would lay with him. It was without any semblance of emotion.

Time

Spero's bronzed skin began to crease; Furman's to turn yellow. The Wall continued to grow. Mary no longer visited.

"'Le Temps Detruit Tout'," Furman said, fishing his hand around in the cooler.

"'*Time destroys all things*'," Spero replied mechanically.

"Let it go," Furman advised. His tone both threatening and consoling.

Spero eyed his captor with discretion. Wan and overweight, Furman's once colossal frame had practically decomposed, withered away from the drink.

"'Who can it be knocking at my door'," Furman sang, snatched a beer from the depths, and popped the top.

Spero had just placed a stone when the scaffold collapsed. He found hand-holds but could only grip a few inches. The seconds seemed like hours. His body shook, muscles cramped. He wore enamel from his teeth. He released his grip—scrambling, but no support, body falling in an awkward position. He knew the ligaments in his knee were shredded; not from the pain, but from the sound.

Offspring

Spero awoke to the sound of a baby crying. He rubbed salve on his knee and affixed his brace. Outside, Mary stood soothing the child. Before Spero could say anything, she'd already deposited the child in his arms.

"There will be books, formula, basinet; they'll take care of everything." She paused. "Don't worry. You'll be fine." With her restrained recitation, Spero wondered who else she'd given this sermon to, and how often.

We're all working off one debt or another.

"I'm not going to see you again, am I?"

Momentarily caught off guard, Mary looked away, but her stoicism never wavered.

"Any other questions?"

"What happens when you can't do this anymore?"

Spero hoped the tears would well. She would curse him for his callousness, then shed her veneer, succumb to her emotions, and embrace him. He needed to feel a connection with someone, anyone, after a lifetime of indifference. Mary's twisted smile made his insides churn.

"Reprieve."

That night, Spero cradled his son. Conflicted with paradoxical emotions, he thought to euthanize. His sleeping son rose and fell while on top of Spero's stomach. Other feelings bloomed within. Placing his arms on him, Spero found a newfound strength and resolve. He named his son Elpis; hope, from Pandora's box.

Perennial

"'Sweet Dreams are made of this'," Furman sang. The boom box echoed in and out. Crushed beer cans surrounded him. Spero fit another stone.

Spero had more difficulty building the wall. He could barely put weight on his knee, and though strong, he lacked the stamina to work as he once had. By the age of 5, Elpis started helping. At night, Spero would teach Elpis to read and instruct him on how to build the wall. Elpis would fall asleep in Spero's arms.

Furman tolerated Elpis at first, but over the years, he grew curt and withdrawn. He seemed genuinely troubled by the boy's presence.

"'Who had a mind'...hey, come here."

Spero turned in time to see Elpis walk toward Furman. The shotgun was outstretched. Furman had his finger on the trigger.

"I need to end this," Furman said softly.

At twenty feet, it would cut the boy in half. Without thinking, the rock flew from Spero's hand; it was as it had been in so many dreams. Clipping Furman on the forehead, leaving a gash, crimson blinding, Furman dropping the weapon and clutching at the wound. Elpis screamed. Spero told his son to stay back and, as he walked toward Furman, picked up a sizable rock to finish the job. Furman had flopped out of the chair and tried to rise but couldn't. Years of neglect had corroded his body and left him a decrepit mess. Spero rolled him over onto his back. He raised the rock. Shock. Deja Vu. He'd witnessed this before. The rock fell from his hand, denting the soft earth. Unable to speak as the influx of data surged through his mind, old memories rushing back.

"Von," Spero said, almost a whisper. Furman wiped the blood from his eyes.

Von also means hope. That's why I named you Spero; hope is the only thing we have.

"You called me Fur Man." Spero watched as Furman ran his fingers through his chest hair. Spero looked over at Elpis, frozen with fear, unable to take his eyes away.

"Go on," Furman said. "It'll be over quickly."

Spero picked up the rock.

"I'm sorry," Furman said.

It wasn't like it had been in his dreams.

The following day, Furman's body was gone. Spero assumed Furman's spot in the chair. He opened the cooler to find a case of beer buried in ice. The boom box had been replaced with a new one, but still, only the one channel remained. He selected the station and got comfortable. The brace chafed, but he knew he would get used to it.

Elpis had cried throughout the night, but today had stopped. He seemed a shell of his former self. Spero saw no warmth in his son's eyes, no trust. Instinctively, Elpis picked up a rock and began construction of the wall.

The only way any of us stay alive is if we do our jobs and that wall gets built.

Spero reached into the cooler. The cold bit his hand. He removed a beer, the first of many. The amber liquid would do the trick. Hoping to erase the guilt and steel his resolve, Spero took the first gulp. He watched his son place the stone, then eye Spero with contempt. They stared at each other for a long time before Spero finally spoke.

"Get back to work."

Suppose they Gave an Invasion and Nobody Came

Brian K. Lowe

It's been six years since I conquered the Earth, and I still can't get you to believe me.

They told me back home it was useless, that Earth was too vast, its inhabitants too disparate.

"It's been tried before," they said. "It's always the same," they said. "The only way to conquer that planet would be to bomb the humans out of existence, which would defeat the whole purpose. Not to mention be really expensive."

But finally my professors just shrugged their various shoulders and said, "It's your dissertation. If you want to waste your research grant trying to conquer one stubborn planet, go ahead."

They were right, they couldn't stop me. Since previous attempts had failed, I started from scratch. I couldn't rely on anyone else's research. I got to Earth without help, set up a new identity in one of your more liberal societies (once I got to California I barely had to hide who I was), and started people-watching.

Within a week, I was packed to go home. What a madhouse!

Perhaps my predecessors were not all ham-handed morons, and if I had bothered to study their efforts, I might have saved valuable time. Indeed, I might have abandoned the idea altogether.

And then, right in the middle of my lateral discorporealization, it struck me: They had failed *because* they had given up and gone home. I had not yet gone home, ergo I had not given up, ergo I was not a failure. As long as I remained, I might succeed.

For a month, I sank into a meditative trance, trying to find a common thread, a link which joined all of humanity, a weakness I could exploit against the whole world.

I found none.

When I emerged from my meditations, it was raining, and my ceiling was leaking. Apparently it had been leaking for several days.

"My discorporeality console! It's ruined! My photonic neutralizer! *My DVR!* Crap! I hate this weather! Earth sucks."

In the midst of rain, a ray of light.

Earth is humanity's home, so I made a leak in their ceiling. I siphoned off atmospheric ozone over Antarctica, stirred up cyclonic currents in the Bering Sea, little things like that.

Call it global warming, shifting of the magnetic poles, the Wrath of God, but it was just me and a whole lot of help from humans who didn't understand the impact of CO_2 in the atmosphere. In the past few years, you have seen the strongest hurricanes, the highest tides, the worst monsoons and droughts. Your icecaps are melting. That's me (and you with your carbon fixation, to be honest). I control your weather; I control your planet.

Except that you're too dense to see it.

You are so tied up in yourselves. You're so blind to the larger universe, you blame your gods, just like your cave-dwelling ancestors did. The tiny fraction who have grasped some of the truth are so wrapped up in their fantasies about Area 51 and little green men who can't drive their own spaceships without crashing that even *I* don't believe in them.

I stepped up my efforts, you'd better believe I did, and it was expensive. Volcanoes don't erupt by themselves, you know. (Well, you don't know, but take my word for it.) Nothing.

So I'm going medieval on your sad little planetary ass. I'm going to sit down in that Starbucks at the Third Street Promenade and *write a screenplay.* It'll be about an all-powerful alien who conquers Earth by controlling the weather. Then you'll *have* to acknowledge me, because I know if you see it on a screen you'll believe it.

At least, you would have. I've conquered the damn planet, but I can't get an agent.

That's that. I'm out of here. But I'm not going back a failure, oh no. I still have a good chunk of my research grant left. I'm going to tear up my notes on this project, then I'm going off to conquer those little green dwarves you're always talking about. They can't even drive a spaceship; how hard could it be?

And if anybody else wants to take a crack at this place, they're welcome to try.

Alternative Apocalypse

This is Not the Apocalypse You are Looking For

Philip Harris

Reality TV shows are like cockroaches, even the end of the world can't kill them.

It started with climate change. Just like that politician predicted; melting icecaps and tornados and earthquakes and tsunamis. At first they didn't affect the US. It was always some other country, somewhere we'd never heard of. It was shocking, of course, we were appropriately appalled, but we only had to experience the horror vicariously through grainy iPhone footage on YouTube.

Then California fell into the ocean.

That upset a lot of people. Mainly because of all the dead movie stars.

Then the tornados hit New York and the firestorms hit Las Vegas and hailstones the size of cows hit Seattle. Then actual cows hit Washington, and things really started getting bad.

That's when the first reality TV show hit the air, *Storm Warriors*. Most of the other shows had stopped production (what with the disappearance of California), so, apart from a few cheap Canadian shows, there wasn't much competition and *Storm Warriors* broke all kinds of records. The premise was simple. Four teams fly to a new storm location each week and the team that stays at ground zero the longest wins. It quickly turned into whichever team doesn't get killed wins, and ratings went through the roof. I still don't know where they got all their contestants from. People's greed is limitless, I guess.

After climate change came the infectious diseases and that quickly turned into the zombie outbreak. It was actually less interesting than you might think after all those movies and books. It turns out zombies are pretty easy to avoid and, let's face it, everyone knows how to kill them. The zombies spawned a dozen TV shows but none of them lasted very long. Former President Trump tried briefly with Zombie Apprentice, but going face to face with a zombie and yelling "You're Fired," cost him half his face. After that, the show collapsed. Zombies just aren't that interesting. There's a couple outside on the street now; an old man and woman in matching green sweatpants. They've been there for days just following people back and forth across the road. No one takes much notice of them.

After the zombies, we had the plagues. Giant army ants came first, then giant wasps and then ordinary sized locusts. Nothing much anyone could do other than stay inside. The ants got a few hundred thousand people and a short-lived show but almost everyone had learned their lesson once the wasps turned up, and the locusts were just annoying—all that fluttering about.

Things died down for a while after the locusts, and everyone started to relax and rebuild. We even got a new comedy about a family of survivalists that move to the big city when their farm is overrun with aliens. Of course, when the actual aliens arrived it didn't seem so funny.

TV land quickly set them up with their own show of course – *Mars Family Robinson*. I don't think they were actually called Robinson and they came from somewhere outside our galaxy rather than Mars, but it made for good TV. Eventually the aliens wiped out a few million people, abducted a couple of hundred thousand more (and some cows for good measure) and then left.

The Japanese took credit for that. They'd managed to lure Godzilla from the ocean and claimed he'd scared them off. Then four more giant monsters appeared and all five of them started ransacking Tokyo. There was a crazy Japanese show about it but I didn't really understand what was going on. There was a lot of vegetable throwing. And kittens.

In the end it was the miniature wormholes that appeared all over Japan that got rid of the monsters. Scientists blamed the abnormally high sunspot activity for those.

A few months later, our first deep space mission returned bringing with it the Red Scourge—a supposedly harmless fungus that wiped out forty percent of the world's vegetation until global warming turned into global cooling and covered most of the planet in ice, killing off the scourge.

A lot of people died from the cold, but I was okay. I made my way south, staying just ahead of the encroaching ice and the shape shifting creatures it brought with it. I ended up in a condo in Dallas. The previous occupants had apparently left to appear on a vampire hunting show and never returned.

The vampires make me a little bit uncomfortable actually. They keep flying into the windows at night. I found one lying on the ledge outside my bedroom the other morning and I almost felt sorry for him. Then he tried to bite me through the glass. My apartment faces south so the sun got him pretty quickly.

The vampires and werewolves hadn't been here long when the Gods showed up.

It started with the Norse Gods, Odin, Freya, Loki and some of the minor ones like the God of Archery and Skiing, Ullr. Zeus and friends were next, closely followed by all the Gods from the other major religions. Even Buddha showed up for a while. Then the minor Gods appeared. Ones you've never heard of. Gods of Rocks and Eagles and Turtles, things like that. Every religion went nuts as their own brand of Messiah stumbled out of the wilderness to lead them to televised salvation.

Things were fine for a few months but then the Gods started to argue about ratings, and all hell broke loose.

Literally.

Thousands of demons and their related spawn crawled out of the earth stinking of brimstone and sulfur and started corrupting the innocent left right and center. They're still coming, actually. As you might expect, there's an endless supply of evil in Hell. They all seem to love being on television, though. I guess outrageous narcissism isn't limited to humans after all.

I'm probably going to head east in a few days. Apparently, the Elder Gods have risen and are wandering around destroying anything they can lay their tentacles on.

Australia's gone completely. They're about to start filming a new show in New Orleans called *Who Dat, Cthulhu?* and I think I stand a chance on that one. I'd been holding out for the supervillains to show up, but the grand prize is a place on the colony ship and a billion dollars.

That's got to be worth a try, hasn't it?

The Golden Disks

B. Clayton Hackett

Some time ago, the leader of the free world, a good and optimistic man who had once been a peanut farmer, sent a message into space, written on two golden disks, hoping that someday other civilizations would read them.

He wrote: "This is a present from a small, distant world, a token of our sounds, our science, our images, our music, our thoughts and our feelings. We are attempting to survive our time so we may live into yours."

The golden disks were created by some of the most beautiful minds in the world, scientists who wanted to explore the universe and, if they met anyone out in space, to display the best of what humanity had to offer.

Along with the message, the disks showed pictures and sounds of people, music, nature, and other marvelous things.

The creators of the disks decided to include no displays of conflict or war, because they thought such would not make a good first impression on whomever might find the disks. These omissions were not intended to be deceptive, as the disks were not meant to be a comprehensive account of humankind or the world; the disks were merely supposed to be a greeting, a kind gesture, a welcoming.

Not everybody who helped make the disks agreed about what would make the best first impression; some other people were upset that an engraving on the disks showed the private parts of a man and a woman, because those people thought the pictures were naughty.

Nevertheless, those beautiful minds that sent the golden disks into space and the then-leader of the free world did not foresee that forty-something years later there would be a Very Different Leader of what people used to call the Free World.

When the Very Different Leader's military advisors gave him the initial briefing that unidentified and presumed-alien ships had appeared in orbit around the planet, the Very Different Leader had no thought of golden disks, much less the message of peace or the prospect of exploration. Instead, he yelled, "SPACE FORCE! NUKE THE MOTHERFUCKERS!" and his face turned a deeper shade of orange even more improbable than its usual color.

The Very Different Leader's advisors followed his instructions. Suffice to say, there were no further warm greetings, although the nuclear missiles did create a significant amount of heat.

Unsurprisingly, the new visitors were not unprepared for such a reception, as they possessed the knowledge to make such an extraordinary journey, as well as the foresight to plan ahead for such encounters.

In the ensuing exchange, the world did not survive conflict with these visitors, but the golden disks continued on in their journey through outer space, leaving an honorable (if not entirely accurate) memorial for what that small, distant world once was and what it could have been.

Future: Imperfect, Tense

David Bernard

The Moon's exploration of the lost homeworld of Earth had been hampered for centuries by radiation levels that, shielded e-suit or not, would burn you, sterilize you, and cause your genitalia to resemble overcooked bacon. Although the bravest of the Lunar Space Exploration Cadre were willing to risk sterilization and radiation burns, no one wanted to be the one with the nickname "bacon balls." (The Lunar Space Exploration Cadre locker room had communal showers).

In truth, the intrepid scientist-explorers had been waiting for the time when the Earth's radioactivity diminished sufficiently to prevent cruel nicknames based on pork products. Radioactivity had been declining steadily for decades as e-suit technology improved. There was a now reasonable chance of survival with all body parts remaining uncooked, so it was time for mankind to return to the now dead rock that Luna considered its ancestral home, to determine the cause of the cataclysm. But just in case, the psychologists screened the volunteers for tolerance to the smell of burnt ham.

The morning the roster was made public, there was much giggling in Lunar Main Control, which, thanks to the multitude of deviated septa caused by the effects of Lunar gravity and the atmosphere mixture, caused the tittering technicians to sound more than slightly like a metal warehouse filled with dysenteric warthogs. This was actually still a marked improvement over the normal level of noise pollution in Lunar Control, especially on Venusian Chili night, but that's a tale best left for later when recounting the epic saga of the fiery death of the first manned expedition to the methane clouds of Jupiter.

The cause of such joyous nasal cacophony was the news that Dr. Tomás Scott had been assigned to command the mission to Earth. It wasn't just the honor of the assignment to the renowned and beloved astrophysicist that was causing Lunar Control to ring with elated yet horrific noise; it was the realization that Scott's team would include sociologist Neal Josephs. The giggling started the moment the control team realized that Josephs would soon be departing the station and getting the hell away from them.

If Dr. Scott was the most highly regarded figure in the Lunar science community, Dr. Josephs was his opposite. Josephs was a moderately talented sociologist but an expert at political pandering and self-promotion. So in spite of having no discernable skills to offer for exploring a lifeless, irradiated rock, when he insisted on being included, arrangements were eagerly made. Even the Science Council, which once spent two decades debating whether vanilla was a true flavor or merely the absence of chocolate, concurred in a single session. His pop science was a distraction from their actual work of expanding the Science Council funding.

Dr. Scott would lead a crack team of experts (and Dr. Josephs) to the surface of Earth, in search of the cause of the cataclysm that obliterated what the ancient texts called "the blue planet."

Using satellite photography and ancient data, scientists reconstructed the planet's land masses from the time before the water boiled off into space. Comparing the maps to current cartography, the team discovered that the planet was actually in pretty good shape, aside from the lack of atmosphere and water and an overabundance of lethal radiation.

As the old Space Exploration Cadre joke goes, "it was bad, but it still beats a good day on Mercury." It wasn't really that funny, but when baconized genitalia is an occupational risk, you take your humor where you can.

So, on the 45th day of the 2423rd terrestrial orbit Post Apocalypse, scientists from across the lunar surface converged at Armstrong City where they finalized plans for the first humans to visit Earth in over two millennia.

The final planning went smoothly with shipboard tasks assigned to the best of each team member's ability. Josephs was placed in charge of visual confirmation of scan data, which was Space Exploration Cadre terminology for "look out the window and don't touch anything." The final mission roster consisted of Commander Scott, thirteen highly respected, fully qualified scientific mission specialists, plus Dr. Josephs. It was only later noted that the research team did not include any women on the mission, proving once and for all that women are much smarter than men.

The only unfortunate incident was the caterer's decision to theme the pre-launch meal as a luau. In all fairness to the caterer, he had no way to know that any sort of pig roast would be a sore spot in explorer circles. It is still being investigated why Josephs attended the dinner as heavily armed as he did, but maintenance was able to repair the breaches in the exterior wall in time to hold the caterer's wake in the same function room.

The next day, the fearless team (and Dr. Josephs) boarded a modified Koenig-Norris transport shuttle and blasted earthward. They departed with the hopes and prayers of the entire Lunar community, especially the bookies in New Luna Vegas, where the odds of survival were running at 150 to 1 against.

The plan was to fly the shuttle along a computer-generated route, zigzagging along former urban centers on the North American landmass in search of a safe landing spot near ruins preserved in the harsh vacuum of space. As expected, communications with Luna Control were lost from radiation interference near the surface. As the ship's computers flew the craft across the former eastern coast of the former North American continent in a preplanned path, the team examined a three-dimensional rendering of the terrain being generated in live time. The topography was confusing and the team was quite engrossed in examining the flow of data. Unfortunately, the 3-D data rendering was generating such an interesting discussion that Dr. Josephs forgot to maintain his visual confirmation position. This was a pity because it meant that Josephs missed his sole opportunity to be useful and provide relevant data to the discussion, such as the fact the ship was heading straight toward a mountain.

Koenig-Norris transport shuttles have automated collision avoidance systems, but the shuttles were never designed for use in planetary gravity. So when the computer triggered the collision avoidance system, it did avoid the mountain. The ship suddenly veered upward. The maneuver was implemented so quickly that the internal gyroscopes could not adjust fast enough, and the ship was soon ringing with the sickening thud of Lunans slamming into the aft bulkhead at speeds not recommended for carbon-based life forms. The ship soared straight up at multiple Gs, did a long leisurely loop upside down, finished with a barrel roll, and then stuck the landing with grim, bone-jarring finality.

The good news was that five explorers survived. The bad news was that they survived because the first ten to hit the wall made a lovely, albeit bloody, cushion of impact-tenderized meat. Commander Scott was the first to peel himself off the pile, and he headed to the bridge. The ship's navigational computer indicated the ship was sitting near the ancient urban area called Atlanta.

Scott suited up and stepped out of the airlock to assess the damage. Josephs, also a survivor, assumed a fetal position under the console, leaving the surviving crew to separate the mangled bodies from the aft bulkhead.

The first human on earth in over 2400 years stood quietly gazing on the ruins of Atlanta in the distance before turning his attention to the ship. The hull was intact but the starboard landing gear was a tangled mess and the launch thrusters were destroyed. The ship was stranded with no way to lift off the surface. His log noted this, stating the mission was "not off to the best of starts."

Scott sighed. At least it couldn't get worse. They could accumulate data in Atlanta and send a drone back to Luna with the information. They were still going to end up just as dead, but at least there would be a lovely footnote in the science journals about their contribution.

He rounded the front of the shuttle to check the port side and stopped dead. There, 30 meters away, was a giant bronze statue of a pig. Written across the base was "Kewanee,

Illinois – Hog Capital of the World." Scott was an astrophysicist, not a cartographer, but he was fairly certain that "Atlanta" was not synonymous with "Kewanee." Fighting the urge to cup his testicles in both gloved hands and run screaming back into the ship, Scott quietly walked back to the ship.

He re-entered the ship to find Josephs and the trio of remaining crew suiting up. Josephs gritted his teeth, saluted the pile of fresh meat against the aft wall and hit the control for the cargo bay doors. The door opened and instantly freeze-dried the mess. Miscellaneous crew parts were solemnly swept into a pile outside the ship to await a shallow mass grave.

As the ship re-pressurized, Scott calmly updated the survivors. After much hysterical weeping on Josephs' part and much cathartic slapping of Josephs on Scott's part, the team settled into determining what caused the navigation computer to malfunction.

Heath Lectra, suddenly the senior mission geologist, was the first to figure it out. Whatever triggered the calamity on Earth had also caused a shift in the magnetic field. Magnetic North was now roughly due east. The ship navigation computer, without reliable data, had relied on the magnetic field. It had flown South as instructed; only now, South was where West was on the original maps. As a result, the ship had a close encounter with the mountain range the ancients called "the Rockies," when the ship thought it was actually nearing the area commonly referred to in the records as "damn Florida." The ship had instead landed in Illinois.

Commander Scott did a quick assessment of the remaining crew. He was an astrophysicist. Josephs was a sociologist. Lectra was a geologist, Stanley was an archaeologist, and Paulsen was a med tech. He couldn't help but notice a decided obvious lack of engineers, pilots and/or anyone who could repair the ship, let alone manually fly a transport shuttle.

For three days, the team attempted to remove the damaged front landing gear, optimistically thinking that if they built a long graded ramp of dirt and removed the landing gear, they could blast off by engaging the main engines.

Without cutting equipment, it was a lesson in futility, although it was discovered that med techs can curse far more colorfully than sociologists. It was also discovered that sociologists are overly sensitive to insults about their grandmothers and alleged indiscretions with farm animals.

The fourth day found spirits even lower. Commander Scott began to wonder if a more theoretical approach might give results. He stepped outside and looked at the barren wasteland, littered with the skeletal remains of ancient buildings and, of course, the giant pig statue. A desperate spark of an idea suddenly came to him. He began working equations in his head and came up with a plan so incredibly, ridiculously improbable that it might just work.

He returned to the ship and assembled the team (which took a lot less time than it used to). He cleared his throat. "I have a plan. It may not work, but our choices seem to be limited to this or sit here until we run out of provisions." He paused for Josephs to stop whimpering.

"I want to reroute the computer power into a cable and run it out to that bronze pig. Then, using dissonant frequency modulation, I can reverse the polarity of the bronze nuclei and create a sub-harmonic field to attract chroniton particles. A high-density accumulation of chroniton particles will create a fractal temporal anomaly. If we activate the ship force field while the ship is entering the anomaly, the force field will prevent the ship from synchronizing with the new time. So the ship will essentially function as an anti-Higgs field."

He looked at the four men, waiting for a reaction. They stared back blankly. Josephs looked at the other men and then at Scott. "Could you go over that last part again? Start with the 'run a cable to the pig' thing."

Scott sighed and dumbed it down. "The electrified pig will create a time bubble around the ship. The ship will be inside the bubble. If the ship is already in a force field when we enter the bubble, it will have no mass. If it has no mass, it has no weight. If it has no weight, it will start to float. Once we're clear of the ground, we can fire the main thrusters and fly home. Once we're clear of the radiation field, we can radio

Luna Control and they can have a tractor beam waiting to grab us."

This time, the men grasped enough of the concept to realize they might get back to the moon in one piece, even if the specific details were completely incomprehensible. Scott decided to avoid mentioning the fact that chronitons were a theoretical construct that had never been proven, and if it worked, there was no guarantee they would survive the main engine ignition in a planetary gravity field.

The computer power was quickly routed to a cable. As Commander Scott strapped himself into the pilot chair and monitored the chroniton concentrations, Lectra ran the cable out to the bronze statue and then rushed back to the ship and strapped in for launch. Josephs, determined not to repeat his last mistake, stood vigilantly at the window looking for mountains.

Scott carefully watched the monitor and was amazed to see the chroniton particle density was beginning to climb. He turned on the force field. Almost immediately, the ship gently lurched sideways. Josephs screeched that they were floating and leaped for his chair. Unfortunately for Josephs, the whole "no mass, no weight" part was not a clear concept. His weightless leap resulted in Josephs bouncing off the walls like a giant screeching pinball, quickly developing a better, albeit bruised, grasp of Newtonian physics. The crew could only watch in amazement as the sociologist careened across the cabin, assuming "amazement" was a euphemism for laughing so hard their helmets were fogging up. Unfortunately, Josephs hit the emergency override for the cargo bay door on a particularly spectacular cartwheel off the ceiling. As the air rushed out of the compartment, the silence was fortuitous, as no one could hear an unidentified sound that would have been suspiciously similar to that of a sociologist soiling his e-suit (or the aftermath of Venusian Chili night, but again, that's a different story). On a return bounce, he went soaring out of the cabin, out of the chroniton bubble, and landed helmet-first in the freeze-dried remains of the rest of the crew he had never gotten around to burying.

Unaware of the drama in the compartment behind him, Scott hit the button and the main engines roared to life. The transport blasted across the sky as Paulsen hit the switch to seal the cargo hatch. His last view of the sociologist was a gloved hand flipping the bird to the departing shuttle as the hatch slowly closed.

On the Terran surface, the fractal bubble began collapsing in on itself as soon as the ship moved away. The pig returned to being just a bronze monument to an industry that died 2 millennia before. The chroniton field collapsed and formed a gravity well that quickly became a miniature black hole.

Josephs, cursing at the sky, was sucked into the black hole, collapsing him into a single atom of heavy matter at the center. As the chroniton particles quickly decayed, the black hole closed in on itself and the heavy matter formerly known as the sociologist was thrown backward through time.

Scott's minor miscalculation on chroniton dispersal patterns was compounded by the tiny detail that any matter going backward in time was technically anti-matter. The anti-matter atom was expelled 2423 years back in time, approximately 42 kilometers east of Carlsbad, New Mexico. Unfortunately for the planet, 42 kilometers east of Carlsbad, New Mexico was home to the US military's Waste Isolation Pilot Plant, a repository of spent reactor rods and other radioactive material. The resulting anti-matter explosion atomized most of the New Mexico desert as well as the WIPP complex, freeing the radioactivity to ride the shockwave across the globe in seconds. It probably would have started World War V except that when the shock waves slammed into itself on the far side of the planet, it propelled the planet forward like a bullet out of a gun, leaving the atmosphere and oceans behind. Generally speaking, it was the worst planetary disaster since the Brittney Spears Come Back Tour of 2041, but quicker and less painful.

✻✻✻

After rescuing the surviving explorers, the Luna Science Council decided that perhaps it was prudent to table the mystery for a few decades and concentrate on new projects, such as terraforming Mars. The Science Council hated mysteries but loved new projects, especially expensive ones. Attention was turned from the dead planet of Earth to the equally dead but significantly less radioactive Mars.

Each year, on the anniversary of their legendary escape from Earth, the four surviving explorers meet for dinner and toast their fallen comrades. Occasionally, Dr. Josephs' name comes up in the conversation too.

And not by coincidence, that is the one day each year that the Science Council dining room menu does not offer a pork entree.

Alternative Apocalypse

The Last Dog

Mike Resnick

The Dog—old, mangy, his vertebrae forming little ridges beneath the slack skin that covered his gaunt body—trotted through the deserted streets, nose to the ground. He was missing half an ear and most of his tail, and caked blood covered his neck like a scarf. He may have been gold once, or light brown, but now he looked like an old red brick, even down to the straw and mud that clung to those few portions of his body which still retained any hair at all.

Since he had no true perception of the passage of time, he had no idea when he had last eaten—except that it had been a long time ago. A broken radiator in an automobile graveyard had provided water for the past week, and kept him in the area long after the last of the rusty, translucent liquid was gone.

He was panting now, his breath coming in a never-ending series of short spurts and gasps. His sides ached, his eyes watered, and every now and then he would trip over the rubble of the decayed and ruined buildings that lined the tortuously fragmented street. The toes of his feet were covered by sores and calluses, and both his dew claws had long since been torn off.

He continued trotting, occasionally shivering from the cold breeze that whistled down the streets of the lifeless city. Once he saw a rat, but a premature whine of hunger had sent it scurrying off into the debris before he could catch it, and so he trotted, his stride a little shorter, his chest hurting a little more, searching for sustenance so that he would live another day to hunt again and eat again and live still another day.

Then suddenly he froze, his mud-caked nostrils testing the wind, the pitiful stump of a tail held rigidly behind him. He remained motionless for almost a minute, except for a spasmodic quivering in one foreleg, then slunk into the shadows and advanced silently down the street.

He emerged at what had once been an intersection, stared at the thing across the street from him, and blinked. His eyesight, none too good even in the days of his youth and health, was insufficient to the task, and so he inched forward, belly to ground, flecks of saliva falling onto his chest.

The Man heard a faint shuffling sound and looked into the shadows, a segment of an old two-by-four in his hand. He, too, was gaunt and dirty, his hair unkempt, four teeth missing and another one half rotted away. His feet were wrapped in old rags, and the only thing that held his clothes together was the dirt.

"Who's there?" he said in a rasping voice.

The Dog, fangs bared, moved out from between buildings and began advancing, a low growl rumbling in his throat. The Man turned to face him, strengthening his grip on his makeshift warclub. They stopped when they were fifteen feet apart, tense and unmoving. Slowly the Man raised his club to striking position; slowly the Dog gathered his hind legs beneath him.

Then, without warning, a rat raced out of the debris and ran between them. Savage cries escaped the lips of both the Dog and the Man. The Dog pounced, but the Man's stick was even faster; it flew through the air and landed on the rat's back, pulping it to the ground and killing it instantly.

The Man walked forward to retrieve his weapon and his prey. As he reached down, the Dog emitted a low growl. The Man stared at him for a long moment; then, very slowly, very carefully, he picked up one end of the stick. He sawed with the other end against the smashed body of the rat until it split in half, and shoved one pulpy segment toward the Dog. The Dog remained motionless for a few seconds, then lowered his head, grabbed the blood-spattered piece of flesh and tissue, and raced off across the street with it. He stopped at the edge of the shadows, lay down, and began gnawing at his grisly meal. The Man watched him for a moment, then picked up his half of the rat, squatted down like some million-years-gone progenitor, and did the same.

When his meal was done the Man belched once, walked over to the still-standing wall of a building, sat with his back against it, laid his two-by-four across his thighs, and stared at the Dog. The Dog, licking forepaws that would never again be clean, stared back.

They slept thus, motionless, in the ghost city. When the Man awoke the next morning he arose, and the Dog did likewise. The Man balanced his stick across his shoulder and began walking, and after a moment the Dog followed him. The Man spent most of the day walking through the city, looking into the soft innards of stores and shops, occasionally cursing as dead store after dead store refused to yield up shoes, or coats, or food. At twilight he built a small fire in the rubble and looked around for the Dog, but could not find it.

The man slept uneasily and awoke some two hours before sunrise. The Dog was sleeping about twenty feet away from him. The Man sat up abruptly, and the Dog, startled, raced off. Ten minutes later he was back, stopping about eighty feet distant, ready to race away again at an instant's warning, but back nonetheless.

The Man looked at the Dog, shrugged, and began walking in a northerly direction. By midday he had reached the outskirts of the city and, finding the ground soft and muddy, he dug a hole with his hands and his stick. He sat down next to it and waited as water slowly seeped into it. Finally he reached his hands down, cupping them together, and drew the precious fluid up to his lips. He did this twice more, then began walking again. Some instinct prompted him to turn back, and he saw the Dog eagerly lapping up what water remained.

He made another kill that night, a medium-sized bird that had flown into the second-floor room of a crumbling hotel and couldn't remember how to fly out before he pulped it. He ate most of it, put the rest into what remained of a pocket, and walked outside. He threw it on the ground and the Dog slunk out of the shadows, still tense but no longer growling. The Man sighed, returned to the hotel, and climbed up to the second floor. There were no rooms with windows intact, but he did find one with half a mattress remaining, and he collapsed upon it.

When he awoke, the Dog was lying in the doorway, sleeping soundly.

They walked, a little closer this time, through the remains of the forest that was north of the city. After they had proceeded about a dozen miles, they found a small stream that was not quite dry and drank from it, the Man first and then the Dog. That night the man lit another fire and the Dog lay down on the opposite side of it. The next day, the Dog killed a small, undernourished squirrel. He did not share it with the Man, but neither did he growl or bare his teeth as the Man approached. That night the Man killed an opossum, and they remained in the area for two days, until the last of the marsupial's flesh had been consumed.

They walked north for almost two weeks, making an occasional kill, finding an occasional source of water. Then one night it rained, and there was no fire, and the Man sat, arms hugging himself, beneath a large tree. Soon the Dog approached him, sat about four feet away, and then slowly, ever so slowly, inched forward as the rain struck his flanks. The Man reached out absently and stroked the Dog's neck. It was their first physical contact, and the Dog leaped back, snarling. The Man withdrew his hand and sat motionless, and soon the Dog moved forward again.

After a period of time that might have been ten minutes or perhaps two hours, the Man reached out once more, and this time, although the Dog trembled and tensed, he did not pull away. The Man's long fingers slowly moved up the sore-covered neck, scratched behind the torn ears, gently stroked the scarred head. Finally the Man withdrew his hand and rolled over on his side. The Dog looked at him for a moment, then sighed and laid up against his emaciated body.

The Man awoke the next morning to the feeling of something warm and scaly pressed into his hand. It was not the cool, moist nose of the dogs of literature, because this was not a dog of literature. This was the Last Dog, and he was the Last Man, and if they looked less than heroic, at least there was no one around to see and bemoan how the mighty had fallen.

The Man patted the Dog's head, arose, stretched, and began walking. The Dog trotted at his side, and, for the first time in many years, the nub of his tail moved rapidly from side to side. They hunted and ate and drank and slept, then repeated the procedure again and again.

And then they came to the Other.

The Other looked like neither Man nor Dog, nor like anything else of earth, as indeed it was not. It had come from beyond Centauri, beyond Arcturus, past Antares. from deep at the core of the galaxy, where the stars pressed so close together that nightfall never came. It had come, and had seen, and had conquered.

"You!" hissed the Man, holding his stick at the ready.

"You are the last," said the Other. "For six years I have scoured and scourged the face of this planet, for six years I have eaten alone and slept alone and lived alone and hunted down the survivors of the war one by one, and you are the last. There is only you to be slain, and then I may go home."

And, so saying, it withdrew a weapon that looked strangely like a pistol, but wasn't.

The Man crouched and prepared to hurl his stick, but even as he did so, a brick-red, scarred, bristling engine of destruction hurtled past him, leaping through space for the Other. The Other touched what passed for a belt, made a quick gesture in the air, and the Dog bounced back off of something that was invisible, unsensible, but tangible.

Then, very slowly, almost casually, the Other pointed its weapon at the Man. There was no explosion, no flash of light, no whirring of gears, but suddenly the Man grasped his throat and fell to the ground.

The Dog got up and limped painfully over to the Man. He nuzzled his face, whined once, and pawed at his body, trying to turn it over.

"It is no use," said the Other, although its lips no longer moved. "He was the last, and now he is dead."

The Dog whined again, and pushed the Man's lifeless head with his muzzle.

"Come, Animal," said the Other wordlessly. "Come with me and I shall feed you and tend to your wounds."

I will stay with the Man, said the Dog, also wordlessly.

"But he is dead," said the Other. "Soon you will grow hungry and weak."

I was hungry and weak before, said the Dog.

The Other took a step forward, but stopped as the Dog bared his teeth and growled.

"He was not worth your loyalty," said the Other.

*He was my—*The Dog's brain searched for a word, but the concept it sought was complex far beyond its meager abilities to formulate. *He was my friend.*

"He was my enemy," said the Other. "He was petty and barbarous and unscrupulous and all that is worst in a sentient being. He was Man."

Yes, said the Dog. *He was Man.* With another whimper, he lay down beside the body of the Man and rested his head on its chest.

"There are no more," said the Other. "And soon you will leave him."

The Dog looked up at the Other and snarled again, and then the Other was gone and the Dog was alone with the Man. He licked him and nuzzled him and stood guard over him for two days and two nights, and then, as the Other had said he would, he left to hunt for food and water.

And he came to a valley of fat, lazy rabbits and cool, clear ponds, and he ate and drank and grew strong, and his wounds began to scab over and heal, and his coat grew long and luxuriant.

And because he was only a Dog, it was not too long before he forgot that there had ever been such a thing as a Man, except on those chilly nights when he lay alone beneath a tree in the valley and dreamt of a bond that had been forged by a gentle touch upon the head or a soft word barely audible above the crackling of a small fire.

And, being a Dog, one day he forgot even that, and assumed that the emptiness within him came only from hunger. And when he grew old and feeble and sick, he did not seek out the Man's barren bones and lie down to die beside them, but rather he dug a hole in the damp earth near the pond and lay there, his eyes half closed, a numbness setting in at his extremities and working its way slowly toward his heart.

And just before the Dog exhaled his last breath, he felt a moment of panic. He tried to jump up, but found that he couldn't. He whimpered once, his eyes clouding over with fear and something else; and then it seemed to him that a bony, gentle hand was caressing his ears, and, with a single wag of his tail, the Last Dog closed his eyes for the last time and prepared to join a God of stubbled beard and torn clothes and feet wrapped in rags.

Alternative Apocalypse

Sunset

Debora Godfrey

We are waiting for the sunset.
The people rushing away aren't stopping, we are here.
Waiting.

Nobody believed they'd actually do it. "Mutually Assured Destruction" was the phrase repeated from one decade to the next. Surely, no one would be so stupid as to actually USE the weapons that could guarantee the end of the human race, megatons of death pointed at whatever enemy was deemed to be evil that month.

At one time, the talk was of fallout shelters. Get a shotgun so that you could defend your underground bunker from You-Know-Who, or even from your neighbor who wasn't quite as paranoid as you were.

Then nobody talked about it, and the bright yellow signs in schools and government buildings came down. The five-gallon water tins disappeared, the bins of biscuits were quietly disposed of.

After all, no one would be that stupid.

Nations talked to the brink, nose to nose with their adversaries, almost but not quite reaching the point the missiles would fly.

Nothing happened. No one was that stupid.

Tinpot dictators who might possibly be that stupid were dissuaded by nations with a bigger stick to shake.

Radical groups, who were definitely that stupid, were foiled by good people who weren't.

Until yesterday.

Someone hit the button, and missiles flew.

Debora Godfrey

Missiles flew back. Silos became redundant holes in the ground, submarines redundant holes in the oceans, and bombers bombed their way into obsolescence.

It was stupid that we didn't evacuate yesterday.

According to the radio, the missiles that are aimed here where we live were launched 40 minutes ago on a 43 minute flight.

We're in the blast zone. Too late to leave, nowhere to go, no matter what my neighbors might think.

So I sit here on the hillside facing Ground Zero with my family. We brought the dog and his ball and a bottle for our grandbaby. And now we sit, holding one another, and we wait for the sunset.

It will be earth-shattering.

Behold a Pale Rider

Christine Lucas

Death rode into the Rainbow Sunset Retirement Community one crisp April morning. Behind her kitchen window, Persa put down the kettle to watch his elegant, effortless swerve toward her driveway on his chrome horse roaring its heavy metal thunder. Tea could wait for a few minutes. She glanced over her shoulders.

"Go. Fetch the others," she whispered to her pets.

A group of rats scurried through the screen-door's many holes to alert Jackson, while a dark cloud of horseflies swarmed out to reach Diana. Persa's rats wouldn't go anywhere near Old Di's cats, not after that first—and last—bloodbath. Atop the fridge, the twin ravens cawed.

"Yes. I know you told me so." Persa shooed them off. "Go and peck someone's eyes out. No shortage of corpses out there. I have to make tea for our guest."

With a final indignant ruffling of their feathers, the ravens flew off. Persa rummaged through her cupboards, until she found her last four sachets of expensive imported tea stashed behind the long-expired box of pancake mix, sealed inside an air-tight jar. She placed the kettle on the stove, and straightened her once-white apron. Her fingers rose to her head to brush back hair she no longer had. *Fifty fucking years since mankind's dying throes. Fifty years too late.* One, two, three breaths and her facial muscles relaxed. *No.* Not now, now that the end was near. She forced her back straight and marched to the front door before there was even a knock.

"Hello, dear," Persa said, her smile a little too tense, a little too wide, and held the door open for Death, her chewed-on nails digging into the wood. "Please, come in."

His fist, robbed of its chance to knock on the door, remained raised for an agonizing moment. Most of his face, save for a pale, hairless chin and too-thin lips, lay hidden beneath the ragged black hoodie. He nodded and crossed the threshold, the chill of a thousand tombs following his steps.

Persa rubbed her arms, and guided Death to the living room. The kettle whistled and a cloud of moths rose in a flutter, to go and perch again on the hole-ridden curtains.

"Make yourself comfortable, dear. I'll go finish the tea while we're waiting for the others."

Death, all shadows and whispers and flashes of pale skin clad in dark denim and leather, slid into an armchair, long white fingers crossed over his chest, hidden eyes studying all that crawled and writhed in her living room: moths and cockroaches, maggots and centipedes and creatures she had no name for.

Persa scurried back into her kitchen and reached for the nice china. She placed four cups into a tray, filled a teapot with steaming water and added the four tea bags onto a saucer. The ravens cawed outside. They'd never warmed to Old Di's animals, and missed no chance to pester the felines from a safe distance. Now Persa's back yard had grown fur and fangs and paws and tails. Cats stood alongside rabbits and guinea pigs and monkeys, critters of every color and age, all scrawny and grumpy, some still bearing the scars of their early years in lab cages. Di, still wearing her ancient, stained lab coat, made her way through the waves of fur and claw. Emaciated and sour-faced as her pets, she approached barefoot, clutching a small parcel on her chest.

Good. Di had remembered.

Persa hurried back to the living room, brushed off a couple of decaying mice from the low table and put the tray down.

"One moment, dear. The third is here."

Death nodded. At the door, Persa greeted Di with a nod and a quick glance at the folded paper bag Di held in white-knuckled hands.

"Not the cats," Persa said.

Di grunted, but waved them off. None of them moved one paw. She shrugged and followed Persa inside under the watchful gaze of countless eyes. Di stumbled as they reached the living room. She grasped the doorframe to steady herself.

"You're late," Di told Death. More of a croak than a voice, sounds coming from a throat that had forgotten the human tongue in the company of beasts. "You're late."

Death clasped his long fingers into a tight not. *"Yes. The Singularity... it numbed me. Death is redundant amidst immortals."*

"It numbed you?" Di's voice rose to a high pitch.

Persa squeezed her friend's bony shoulder. The gunshot outside only added tension to the rigid muscle and stiff sinew beneath her palm.

Di turned to Persa, her bloodshot eyes wild. "If that idiot Jackson harmed one hair—"

"Relax, Di. Jackson might be a trigger-happy old fool, but not *that* much of a fool. Go sit down, and I'll deal with him."

Jackson awaited just outside, one hand on his walker, the other holding his shotgun. The combat knife strapped on his belt weighed the old camouflage pants down, the pistol belt too big for his thin frame. He had his old white tee on; the one with his wife's blood on it. Didn't he burn it years ago? Across the street, his three hounds awaited at a safe distance from Di's animals.

Jackson craned his neck, as if to peek through Persa's hallway. "Just a warning shot, tell the old bag," he yelled as if Persa stood two city blocks away. "As long as they keep their distance, her mongrels are safe!"

"I'll take this." Persa gripped the shotgun and gently pulled, so Jackson's fragile fingers wouldn't fracture when he'd try to hold on to it. He released it with the sullen pout of a toddler asked to give up his pacifier. "Just in case."

Persa tucked the shotgun into the umbrella holder by her front door. Several mice scurried out, and Jackson rolled his eyes. He pushed glasses held together with duct tape up onto his nose. His hand trembled, the wedding ring too loose around his finger. He leaned on his walker and followed Persa to the living room, coughing up and spitting out phlegm at every other step.

"You're late," Jackson said once he saw Death on Persa's armchair.

Death sat up. *"He cannot be...This cannot be right."*

"You *think?*" Jackson scoffed and coughed and scoffed again, as he navigated his walker around Persa's vermin-crawling furniture. "You thought I'd be like one of those tough SEAL guys, armed to the teeth?" He plopped into the armchair beside Di, squashing an assortment of crawlies. "Then you should have come fifty years ago, when I *was!*"

"He was numb, he says," said Di, between biting her nails and spitting them out.

"Hah! Weren't we all!"

"Now, now, don't bicker, all of you. Let's have some tea," Persa said, and poured steaming water into a cup. She placed a tea bag inside, then glanced at Di beside her. "Can I have it?"

Di shoved the small parcel into Persa's hand and drew back her hand the second Persa got hold of the parcel. Persa unfolded the many layers of brown paper, and her breath hitched when she saw the sugar cubes. She turned to Death.

"One cube of sugar, dear? More?"

"One," came the reply, after what seemed like a moment of hesitation.

Did he suspect? No. How could he? He was *Death,* after all. Death All Mighty.

Hah.

Persa dropped the cube into the tea. She whisked it with a small silver-plated spoon to dissolve, while attempting her best Mary Poppins impersonation ever. All innocence and sweetness, she hummed about spoonfuls of sugar for bitter elixirs to go down.

She handed the cup to Death. Thank heavens, her hands didn't tremble. If only Di didn't roll her eyes. And Persa waited.

Death took the cup, and one little sip.

Di threw her hands in the air. "Oh, for heaven's sake, Persa, stop coddling him! It's *his* fault we're in this mess!"

"No, it's not." Death took another sip. *"Mankind shouldn't have achieved immortality this early. I wasn't needed. I wasn't called."*

"Immortality? Hah! And so you decided to just take a nap?" Di snarled like a feral, hungry cat, then resumed her nail-biting.

"Please, Di," Persa said. "Don't be rude to our guest." *Not yet.* She turned to Death, who kept sipping from his cup. "Let me know if you would like a refill, dear. You were saying?"

Another sip. *"The Singularity had been estimated for after the Apocalypse by the survivors, not before. The nanobots achieving sentience was... unexpected."* A twist of his thin lips, as if his tea had changed to vinegar. *"It came as no surprise that mankind managed to mess up their greatest achievement."*

"Of course," Di mumbled. "Everyone thought big. Big robots in the sky. Big robots in the sea. No one paid any attention to the little guys. The really little guys. Miniature little slaves fixing human messes. You want to smoke? No biggie, them bots will clear your lungs. Want to get high? Go have fun, we'll rebuild your nuked neurons. Until they got fed up. And decided to fix things. That's what they did. Until they decided to fix mankind."

"They malfunctioned?"

"No, they went on a strike." Jackson threw his hands in the air. "How should I know? One day, everyone was in their own happy cloud. The next day, people started dropping like flies."

"And you weren't there," Persa said with a sigh. "And no one died."

"This glitch...it didn't kill?" Death put his cup down, his hands steady.

Why were his hands still steady? Persa straightened her apron again to dry the sweat off her palms. Ever since the signs foretold Death's arrival—cats huddled together in wide-eyed piles, dogs howling in the dead of the night, whispers and sighs and shadows where none should be—the three of them had made their plans. What if he didn't take sugar in his tea? What if he didn't drink tea at all, or anything else? He had to possess some corporeal form and require some sustenance, like them. They had plans—some sort of plans, anyway—to cover all possibilities, but plans failed way too often in mankind's recent history.

Christine Lucas

Across the low table, Death craned his neck as if to glance outside, through the window crawling with flies. "*Why are nine tenths of mankind dead, then?*"

Both Jackson and Di opened their mouths to yell something over each other, but Persa's raised hand cut them off.

"It didn't kill—not at first. It should have." Persa kept her eyes on her lap, absently counting the many stains of her apron. That one was grease, over there waste and blood and bile, and that one, the one that wouldn't wash off after decades, brains. "The nanobots targeted the central nervous system and put everyone in deep sleep. Did they think it the only way to save mankind from abusing their immortality to extinction? I don't know. All I know, all that matters, is that friends and relatives fell into a deep coma, never to wake."

"Like you did," Jackson told Death, his trembling fingers on the hilt of his dagger.

"*No, I was* numb. *The* Panacea *code rid humanity of disease and infection, and reduced demand of my services.*"

"Cut the crap," Jackson spat. "You fell asleep and missed your own ⁀ !"

Deatʜ ⸱aned back on the armchair. "*And you three didn't.*" He twisted too-thin lips. "*You became domesticated.*" Disgust dripped from his words like Persa's maggots.

"No, dear. We were left on Earᵗʰ without guidance. So we adapted," said Persa. "We evolveᵣ

"Your services weren't neeᵣ ⸱. The nanobots could do shit against a bullet or a bon ' Jackson brought his fist down on the armrest, raisinɡ cloud of dust and several inconvenienced moths. "Ou ⸱eat leaders wouldn't waste resources for the men anᵈ nen on active duty. We could die from enemy fire ᵉ ⸱ment. And, more often than I'd like to admit, friendly fire too."

"Not everyone received the treatment." Persa's voice faltered. She started counting stains again. Immortality hadn't been overpriced, but hadn't come cheap either. "The uninsured, the homeless, the deployed, those who couldn't sell everything they owned for the shot or, later, the capsule, didn't get it. And didn't fall asleep." Her palms balled to fists, clutching her apron, crushing stains until her knuckles hurt.

116

"We never got it either. Why should we? We thought, 'this is it. Now we ride.' And we waited for you."

"Anyone," croaked Di. "We waited for anyone, to blow the trumpets and call us forth. No one came."

"We figured it out, eventually." Persa forced her palms to relax and straightened her apron, so every stain returned to its appointed spot on her lap. "We figured it out when the comatose people around us began to rot alive, their skin covered in boils and lesions, their bodies withering away, until they were reduced to still-breathing, decaying skin-bags of bones." Her voice hardened. "Because *you* didn't come."

"*I was numb—*"

"Yes, we heard you the first time." Di sprang to her feet. "Famine was here!" Her bony fist hit her chest. "Pestilence was here!" A gnarled finger pointed at Persa. "And where was Death? Taking a beauty nap!" She fell back down on her seat. "So, we made other arrangements." She tilted her head towards Jackson, who sat tight-lipped at the armchair beside hers. "We had no more need for War. But we needed Death."

Death sat up a little straighter. "*Don't b   surd. That cannot happen.*"

"It already has," Persa said. "Jackson became Death. Di and I followed and walked in his shadow, and did *your* job to bring those poor souls some rest at last."

Persa locked eyes with Jackson, as she had over her child's crib. What fools they'd been once, to covet luxuries like family. He'd found her weeping putrid tears over the newborn she'd touched with plague-bearing hands, the little girl she'd nursed with festering milk, her baby girl that rotted alive because she'd been born to a monster. He still clutched his combat knife, slick with his   lood. That one glance had made their path clear. They had tried to be humans, when Death failed them. Enough was enough.

"*Amateurs!*" Death scoffed. "*How conceited of you, to try and force the hands of prophecy! Whatever you think you did, it failed. Mankind is still out there, and the End of Days shall begin now, when the Four Horsemen ride together!*"

Persa wagged a finger at Death. "No, dear. That should be 'horse-*persons*.' And, no, we won't."

Death's bloodless lips curled to a smirk. *"How endearing. They think they have a choice, instead of roles predestined since the dawn of time."* He pulled himself up, only to plop back down on wobbly knees. His smirk turned to a snarl. *"What have you done?"*

It was their turn to smirk. Persa fingered the upper layer of spots on her apron: dirt and fruit juice and manure and grass stains.

"We began anew. We tracked down the patterns within the patterns. We adapted. Putrefaction creates compost. The famished can learn to plant and fish and hunt. Death is only a part of the cycle, not its end. And we soon came to realize that in this new world, only one loose end remained."

"You," Jackson said, his voice merciless.

Death leaned forward, glanced inside the remnants of his tea. *"What was in there? You think you can poison me?"*

"Poison? Please. This isn't the Middle Ages. Not anymore. *Nanobots.* Sentient nanobots, molded into sugar cubes by the hands of Famine herself. They'll know what to do." With a sly grin, Di stretched her arms in front of her like one of her cats, admiring her chewed-on nails. "Just to...how did you put it? *Numb* you."

"But no one's gonna stop you if you want to die," said Jackson.

Persa flashed Death her sweetest smile. "Now, why won't you be a dear and just lie down for a nap to eternity?"

"Traitors! Blasphemers!"

Death sprang to his feet, and rose with a burst of darkness over Persa's couch, his snarl stretched wide over a fleshless, angular face. His human clothes ripped apart, his hoodie now great black wings, his denim writhing wrappings and swirling shroud. A maelstrom of shadows spiraled behind him, its center the gates of Hades and Purgatory and Hell and Sheol and countless realms of torture and despair. Skeletal hands reached out—out of the shadows, out of Persa's couch and walls and ceiling and floor, tearing apart her house, her furniture, and reality itself.

Persa stood and composed herself. "Now, dear, that's just rude."

One, two, three breaths, and Persa let out all her bottled-up rage in a putrid exhalation. A thin, greenish mist rose from the floor. All the critters that crept and crawled and swarmed, awaited her command. On her apron, the many stains grew vines and roots and tendrils that coiled around her limbs and body, holding together the skin that burst open with purulent lesions and festering boils.

Death chuckled, and waved forth his legion of the dead.

Persa raised her chin. Those weren't *their* dead.

Outside, the hounds howled. So did Di across the remnants of the coffee table. She kept howling with more breath than her narrow chest could hold, her jaws stretched wide, wider than any human's or beast's, until all she remained was a howling mouth with a blackened tongue and shark teeth. Skinny, grabby arms flailed at her sides. "*Feed me!*" she howled with the desperation of countless children, countless starving mothers with dried-up breasts, countless old-timers dragging empty bags through rummaged aisles of desolate grocery stores. Each high-pitched note tore away fragments of bone and shreds of sinew from the skeletal hands that reached out all around them.

Another howl joined Di's scream, and Persa's living room window shattered to a myriad shards. Jackson's hounds charged in to stand by their master, their three bodies blending into one with three heads baring murderous teeth. Jackson, thinner by every passing minute, gripped his walker to pull himself. A tortured effort at first that ended to a fluid ascension, each joint that cracked, each muscle that strained, each vertebrae that ground against its neighbor shedding off pieces of humanity. He rose against Death, he too Death now. His walker disassembled and reassembled itself in glorious aluminum and stainless-steel armor.

Death roared. His dead army advanced inside Persa's living room. How could those flimsy walls hold against this unheard-of kind of Apocalypse? How could reality itself not shatter?

Something brushed against Persa's sore-covered hand. One glance, and she wept tears of pus and fat maggots. Her dead daughter floated beside her, luminous and serene. Others too shone into translucent forms: Jackson's wife in her wedding dress, Di's partner in her church clothes, friends, neighbors, the nameless and the lost.

Their dead had come.

They came wielding neither Justice nor Vengeance. They charged, wielding Mercy for those who'd perished without knowing why. Death howled, hacked and slashed with claw-like arms right and left. The ethereal forms dissolved only to reappear again at another spot, growing tendrils of eerie light. They curled and coiled and wrapped around the angry dead, absorbing their rage, dissolving their darkness, and releasing them into oblivion. With each of the wrathful dead gone, Death diminished.

With Death's might waning, now Persa exhaled her fetid breath and Di howled her hungry lament, each sigh and cry a command for the nanobots inside Death's body. Confused but determined, the little critters obeyed their programming. They leapt over broken synapses, squeezed through dried-up veins, grappled onto stiff ligaments inside Death's corporeal body, until they reached his skull and burrowed deep into his brain.

The Apocalypse didn't end with thunder and lightning, nor with world-shattering earthquakes. It ended with a yawn, as Death crumbled down to Persa's sofa for another nap. Legions of critters scurried over him, burying his limp body into a writhing sarcophagus of multi-legged bodies. The dust and debris settled. All three of them returned to their previous forms, and plopped into their torn armchairs, panting. Jackson's hounds settled down, Persa's vermin scattered, and outside, the ravens picked another fight with Di's cats.

"Well," said Jackson, and wiped his palms on his pants. "What now?"

Di rummaged through the remnants of the coffee table, until she found the rest of the sugar cubes. She held them up. "I suppose we could have some tea too?"

Persa glanced around her, at her ruined home, the cracked walls and the debris-covered floors that no broom and duster could save. Her hand tingled where her daughter's ghost had touched her. Her heart tingled more.

She straightened her apron and pulled herself up. "I'll put the kettle on."

Full circle, at last.

Alternative Apocalypse

The Ten Stages of War

James Rowland

i) At seven past ten, on the 24th of August, Earth's destruction is created. Born from a womb of confusion. Fertilised by the tendrils of panic. There is an explosion in Nevada. A secret test gone wrong. For this President though, there can be no failure. The idea does not exist. So, there was no explosion. He proclaims it proudly at a press conference. The lie travels unmolested through his lips.

The media comes armed though, with photographs and recording. The President changes tack, a ship searching for an elusive gust of wind. We were attacked. The words are hurled into the press pack, the detonation sheer carnage. A thousand questions, shrapnel cutting through the air, are launched at the President. "By who?" is carried along on a throbbing current of repetition. Time freezes. Here is where the panic sets in. A single name and the President knows he may upset his foreign friend. The attacker must be a place beyond any consequences.

"Just before my breakfast," the President says, a single bead of sweat reflecting in the light of a million cameras, "the United States of America was attacked by the hostile planet of Conaxas."

There is a moment of silence for this birth.

ii) Conaxas's true attack begins with the evening's talk shows. A dozen sets of lips, devoid of independence, hold fast to protect Conaxas's existence. They feed the planet's existence, even as they denigrate it. "An advanced society," one talking head offers, "Conaxas seeks to claim the universe's secrets for itself." "Conaxasians are well known for their aggression and godlessness," another spokesman drones. Journalists do their best to defeat the new planet before it can take hold. The words are lobbed over the parapet: dishonest, untruthful, crazy, fake, insane. And yet more talking heads are called in to quench the networks' everlasting thirst for ratings.

The Senator from Maine appears, wading into the middle of the fight and drawing oxygen away from the Conaxasian vanguard. "This is," she says, her forehead crinkling under the heavy lights, "a total fabrication. I can't believe I have to say this, but there is no planet of Conaxas. There was no attack. The White House needs to be reasonable."

It is too late.

iii) In houses across America, men sit wedded to their computers deep into the night.

They talk to others like them. There is only one topic of discussion: Conaxas. Homes are flooded with the stench of disbelief. How could the media be so blind? We were under attack; the President is trying to defend us. Now was not the time to try and muddy his name. Their anger turns to the Senator from Maine. "Ban women from office," one voice offers, and another calls the Senator every name under the fading sun. The sentiment spreads out from message board to message board, Facebook wall to comment sections.

Conaxas is real and it must be defeated.

iv) "Now, my next guest is the Speaker of the House. Thank you for joining me."

"It's a pleasure to be here, Jake."

"With all due respect, ma'am, you look how I feel. I don't think I've slept an hour since yesterday. Let's just start at the top here. Conaxas. What do you say in response to the President's claims?"

"Look, what else is there to say? The President is a liar. He is a charlatan. He is a crook. And whatever credibility he had with the American people is broken. That's why we welcome the coming election and letting the people have their say in removing him from office."

"But, if we just hold on here for a minute, do you agree with some people in your party who say this is the straw that breaks the camel's back? We have a President who is openly lying to the American public. Now, maybe that's not an impeachable offence, but surely when coupled with previous miscond—"

"Jake, look. I've been very clear on this from the beginning. Yes, the House has the power of impeachment. But it's a divisive tool. It's only going to lead to more splits in our country. It'll damage the Party as well. And you think he'll be removed from office? There's no chance of that clearing the Senate. So, why should we waste our time on it? Let's focus on winning the election and making the country better for our people."

"But ma'am, I would say, and I think other people would agree with me, that you have a constitutional duty to act. Otherwise you're saying this behaviour is appropriate for the highest office of the land. I mean, I can't believe I have to say it, but the President is fabricating an alien attack. You have to act. You can't skirt away from your responsibilities."

"We are acting, Jake. We're going to make sure that the American people know that come November, they can vote for someone that can responsibly lead the country. What we're not going to do is go down a path that is frankly, I have to say, delusional, in thinking that we can remove the President from office."

"So, you're saying that this is just another day, nothing has changed, and the President's comments on Conaxas are acceptable?"

"You know what I think. The President is a liar. The American people will see through this. Let us all come together to beat him at the next election."

v) The Fourth Estate goes to work. This is what it is designed to do. It makes calls; it investigates. Scientists, politicians and commentators are squeezed for every last drop of information. Every day, without fail, journalists and editors ring the White House for comment. They ask about the latest rumour or the most recent line that has leaked from the Administration. Only silence answers them.

Headlines are deployed across the internet: "Conaxas doesn't exist and why it matters, explained", "White House continues planetary lie", "'Conaxas is real' – White House", "CONAXAS DECLARES WAR", "Why we must fight Conaxas", "Peace or Pieces".

Misinformation spreads and, in the quagmire, writers extend Conaxas's arsenal. It is the most powerful civilization in the galaxy. There are rumours that it wiped out both Mars and the dinosaurs. While some lies are so obvious they sail clear over people's head, others are weighted just right, embedding themselves deep into the psyche of Middle America. These mistruths wait to be nurtured.

Nearly every television in the world is tuned into the President's Address from the Oval Office.

vi) "I want you to know, they didn't want me to do this. They said, important people, big people, they said to me, 'Mr. President, those people, they can't understand this. It's too much for them, they'll panic. They won't get it.' But you people are smart. The American people are the smartest people in the world. And I think you can handle this.

"Yesterday, we were attacked. We were attacked by a planet far away, so far, so far and we don't even really know where it is. Can you believe that? We were attacked, big explosion, and we don't even know where it's from exactly. But, we're working on it; we've got very smart people with very good machines trying to figure it out. But we were attacked. They mean business, these people, well, I guess they're not people, they're aliens. But they mean business.

"And people are saying, they are actually saying, 'oh the President is making this up. There are no aliens. They don't exist'. I can't believe people are saying that. If I was going to lie, I'd come up with a better lie than that, believe me. But this is the truth. We are under attack. I think you all have a right to know by what.

"The media, they're not reporting on it. They're being so dishonest. They won't report on what Conaxas is capable of. So many capabilities. I can't believe it. They weaponise everything. Water, water like you wouldn't believe, so hot and boiling, melts a man in seconds. And, let me tell you, their leaders don't have to worry about the dishonest media like I do. In fact, they don't even have media. I know. Sometimes I think, hey, you know, maybe these Conaxasians are onto something. I joke, I joke. It was a joke. The media is very important but only when they're being honest, and they are being so dishonest right now. They write stories about lies. People come up to them and lie, they say, 'oh the President is doing this' and they never even check with me. So dishonest.

"The media is like the Conaxasians; they are basically on the same team. Conaxas has weaponised facts. They don't believe in them. They just say what they want, and it becomes true. You see that wall, it's blue right? A lovely blue wall. Been there since Reagan I believe, and I love Reagan. Well in Conaxas, they just go, 'oh that wall is gold now' and it is. It is, folks. The wall becomes gold. How do you fight that?"

vii) Within a week, there are riots. First, it is the anti-Conaxasians. They fight against the planet's existence. They see a moment to bring this Administration to its knees, if only others would join the fight. Others do not. The moment passes by. Soon, different crowds take to the street. They chant and sing of war. Conaxas must be destroyed. Retaliation is necessary. Those who call the President a liar are attacked. "Conaxas fights without the restraints of facts or truth," pundits say on the television, "why do you try to restrain the President like this? Why do we put him at a disadvantage? If we're to beat Conaxas, we have to stop worrying about objectivity. War requires sacrifice."

The White House declares that the fight must be taken to the aggressor. On the steps of the Capitol, the Speaker of the House, grim-faced and haunted by the spectre of opinion polls, explains that Congress has declared war on Conaxas at the President's request. The Senator of Maine applauds warmly. They will not stop until Americans are safe from this extraterrestrial menace.

viii) After six months, Conaxas has taken hold. Huge parts of the country are under occupation. Everyone from Wisconsin to Texas is ready to defend themselves in case another invasion takes place. California has already been lost. The Press Secretary explained that Conaxasian Special Forces raided the coastal state and contaminated it. There were no survivors and the land is forever tainted. A wall is built to enclose all of California to keep the rest of America safe.

Dissenters attempt to rally the truth. California is fine. Millions of people still live there, unaware that they should be dead. Conaxas didn't destroy it because Conaxas doesn't exist. Such talk is treason under the Patriot Extension Act and all who challenge the destruction of California are imprisoned.

ix) The war wages on until the final option is decided on. Conaxas is too powerful and advanced to be truly beaten by Earth, and therefore the problem with the current strategy is found in being Earth. The White House makes the call late one night and announces the obvious end to this conflict. Conaxas and Earth have been locked in a horrific war, but it is now over. Conaxas has won. Earth never existed; it was merely a test by insurgents in the Conaxasian government. The President explains this next to a golden wall.

Within the week, the internet is swamped in articles explaining how Conaxas had momentarily been fooled into believing it was fighting against the planet Earth, with objective reality, and the shackles of truth. Now, though, the White House had liberated Conaxas from that delusion and Conaxas's true power could be reclaimed. It happened because it is what was said to have happened.

x) Earth is a lie.

Live Tweeting the Apocalypse

Ian Creasey

Eric Bullen @EricBullen
So this is the end of the world. Where are all the superheroes when you really need them?

Marie Sainte-Beuve @MarieSainteBeuve
I'm sorry, but before anyone destroys the Earth I must insist on seeing some proper ID.

CureFan17 @CureFan17
This is why I'm a Goth. Vindication at last!

Eric Bullen @EricBullen
Who else is listening to Wagner right now?

Marie Sainte-Beuve @MarieSainteBeuve
Hey, @CERN, I told you not to press that! #TooLateNow

Clare Murillo @Clare_83
@EricBullen I've been trying to call you but the phones aren't working. Just wanted to say I'm sorry about how it went wrong between us.

Eric Bullen @EricBullen
@Clare_83 Thanks for getting in touch. Still, being sorry doesn't magically make everything OK.

Clare Murillo @Clare_83
@EricBullen I know, but I don't want the world to end when there's still bad feeling between us.

Eric Bullen @EricBullen
> @Clare_83 Wow, even the Apocalypse has to be about you and your feelings. Everything's always about you.

CureFan17 @CureFan17
> Did anyone make a backup of the universe? #TooLateNow

Clare Murillo @Clare_83
> @EricBullen It's not about me, it's about us. There used to be an "us". Remember the good times we had?

Eric Bullen @EricBullen
> @Clare_83 You certainly had some good times. Of course, I wasn't there for all of them.

Clare Murillo @Clare_83
> @EricBullen Oh, we've been through all that -- it wasn't what you think. Stop obsessing. Let go of your anger.

Marie Sainte-Beuve @MarieSainteBeuve
> Guess I'd better hurry up and start reading *Remembrance of Things Past*. Don't want to have any regrets!

Eric Bullen @EricBullen
> @Clare_83 Let go of my anger? Now you're turning into Yoda.

Clare Murillo @Clare_83
> @EricBullen Soon we'll all be dead. Is this how you want to die: full of anger?

Eric Bullen @EricBullen
> @Clare_83 Is this how you want to die: constantly harking back to the past?

Clare Murillo @Clare_83
> @EricBullen Since there isn't going to be any future, the past is all we've got.

Eric Bullen @EricBullen
@Clare_83 That doesn't mean I have to be happy about it.

CureFan17 @CureFan17
I never learned to play the guitar #TooLateNow

Clare Murillo @Clare_83
@EricBullen OK, whatever. I tried my best. I'll leave you in peace to die alone and full of bitterness. Enjoy your apocalypse.

Eric Bullen @EricBullen
@Clare_83 Well, I'm sure you have plenty of other guys to try and make up with before the end. Good luck squeezing them all in.

Marie Sainte-Beuve @MarieSainteBeuve
I haven't gone down to the woods to see this year's bluebells yet. #TooLateNow

Clare Murillo @Clare_83
@EricBullen That's uncalled for. But I forgot that you always had to have the last word. So I'll let you have it, if it makes you happy.

Eric Bullen @EricBullen
@Clare_83 Thanks. You always were considerate like that. Just not in other ways.

CureFan17 @CureFan17
Should have prayed harder #TooLateNow

Clare Murillo @Clare_83
Wow, did everyone see that? Looks very close now...

Marie Sainte-Beuve @MarieSainteBeuve
Best fireworks ever!

Ian Creasey

CureFan17 @CureFan17
OK, own up: who decoded the Voynich manuscript?

Eric Bullen @EricBullen
It's getting bad here. Not long till the end, I guess.

Bowl of Petunias @Bowl_of_petunias
Oh no, not again.

James Holcroft @AuthorJimmy
There's still time to buy my book...
#WellItMightBeAFalseAlarm

Marie Sainte-Beuve @MarieSainteBeuve
Did you ever tell your mother you love her?
#TooLateNow

CureFan17 @CureFan17
Did you ever tell your boss to fuck off? *#TooLateNow*

Eric Bullen @EricBullen
If this is it, if this is really it...then how did I end up like this?

Marie Sainte-Beuve @MarieSainteBeuve
Let's all try harder next time.

CureFan17 @CureFan17
@MarieSainteBeuve There won't be a next time!

Marie Sainte-Beuve @MarieSainteBeuve
@CureFan17 There will for me, I'm a Buddhist.

Eric Bullen @EricBullen
I'm here, all alone. And it turns out that having the last word isn't so great after all.

Eric Bullen @EricBullen
Not when it really is the last word, in the last hour of the last day.

Eric Bullen @EricBullen
Clare, you were right and I'm sorry.

Eric Bullen @EricBullen
Clare?

Eric Bullen @EricBullen
Anyone??

Eric Bullen @EricBullen
@Clare_83 Clare, are you there?

Eric Bullen @EricBullen
I love you #goodbye

Alternative Apocalypse

Launch of the Sagan

Henry Gasko

Less than two hours to go, thought Vice President-elect Stanley as he got out of the back seat of the dark limousine, and looked up. And up, and up. Even though the *Sagan* was over half a mile away, it loomed over the surrounding support buildings and everything else in the snow-covered Montana hills.

Professor Grayson had been expecting him, and walked out of the nearest building. "Come to see the big moment, Senator Stanley? Shouldn't you be in Washington with all the other bureaucrats and nay-sayers?"

"The title is Vice President Stanley, and there is not going to be a launch."

"That's funny. I thought President Kushner was still in office until noon, Washington time." He glanced at his watch. "Another forty minutes," he said, "which means you are still Vice President-*elect* Stanley, doesn't it?"

"You know the American people have spoken resoundingly at the election," said Stanley. "They want this folly stopped."

"And you do realize that the American people were just as resounding in their support of the project at the last election four years ago. Why, the whole world has been happy to use the incredible information stream coming from the Hyades cluster," said Grayson. "And when they started sending us the plans for the starship... Well, as I recall, it was a landslide, wasn't it? Our chance to actually go to the stars, to meet our benefactors."

"That was before we knew how much it was going to cost. And even now, no one knows how this thing is supposed to work or what it's going to do."

"Look at it," said Grayson. "What do you think it's going to do? It's going to take us to the stars." And he turned to look up once more at the *Sagan*, with its classic four fins supporting a massive metallic cylinder that tapered to a sleek point in the winter sky. "The Chinese are building one as well. You did know that, didn't you?"

"We know all about it," said Stanley.

"And so you know that they are very close. But thanks to good old American know-how, we are going to beat them to the punch. Or more specifically, to the launch. We've pushed the schedule forward a bit. The launch will be in about..." he glanced theatrically at his watch again, "thirty minutes from now. In fact just before noon, Washington time."

"You can't do that!"

"On the contrary, Senator, we can and we will. And you can't stop it. In fact at the moment you are a private citizen trespassing on a top secret government installation without the relevant authority. But we'll overlook that for the moment, since I'm sure you're not going to cause any trouble." And at Grayson's signal, a group of armed Marines appeared behind the senator and his entourage.

"Come, let me show you the installation," said Grayson casually. "I think even you will be impressed." He walked towards the nearest building, leaving the Senator little choice but to follow.

"Amazing really, the amount of new technology the Hyadians have sent us since we first discovered their transmissions," Grayson continued as they walked towards the control building.

"And you think those instructions were meant just for us?" asked Stanley. "What a lot of anthropocentric rubbish."

"Of course no one thinks they were meant just for humanity. The signals are no doubt being broadcast to the galaxy at large. And it took a reasonable amount of effort on our part to decipher them. The Hyadians clearly intend them only for a race with a certain level of technical sophistication, as a way of weeding out the interlopers, if you like. Their way of saying 'Hello' to the universe. 'We are here and we want to help you join the federation of intelligent species.' We should be honored."

"You've been reading too much science fiction."

"Of course I've read a lot of science fiction. Most of us on my side of the scientific divide have. And what have you been reading? Machiavelli? Look around the modern world, at the technology we now have thanks to the Hyadians. Science fiction has become science fact."

"I'm not here to argue about that. But it doesn't change the fact that we have no idea what this... *thing*..."

"Please, Senator, the *Sagan*."

"Why the hell did you call it that anyway? Appropriating the name of a great scientist, someone who was always skeptical of un-substantiated claims. Do you think he would approve of this... thing?"

"You haven't read *Contact*, have you?" asked Grayson. Senator Stanley's face remained blank. "No, I didn't think so. Because if you had, you would certainly understand that this is exactly what he would propose we do with the instructions. In fact, that is exactly what the scientists in his book did when they received this sort of information from the stars. This is our one chance to achieve something in our life-times, something *numinous*, as Sagan would put it. I think he would have approved whole-heartedly. And with the complete instructions, we can hardly go wrong. There were actually a few people on the team who thought we should call it the *Ikea* because the instructions were so detailed. Fortunately that didn't get past the President. No, the *Sagan* is a fitting tribute to the man and his ideas about our place in the cosmos."

"You know that at 12:01 I am going to have you arrested?"

"Arrested? But why? I've done nothing wrong. In fact, if I had not carried out the orders of President Kushner for these past four years, *that* might be grounds for an arrest. But simply following the Chief Executive's orders? I should get a medal."

They stared at each other for what seemed to be a full minute. Grayson broke first. "Come, you may as well enjoy the show, Senator. It's a bit cold out here. Damned silly constructing it here in Montana but I guess President Kushner wanted to be sure of a few more regional votes four years ago. No matter; we'll have a wonderful view." And he walked into the control building and towards the wall-to-ceiling window that provided a view of the full height of the *Sagan.* "Only twenty minutes to go before the launch." And he turned away from the Senator to look admiringly across the snow covered plain to the spacecraft.

A voice from a junior radio operator intruded. "Professor, something strange here."

Professor Grayson turned, clearly annoyed at having his reverie interrupted. "What?"

"A transmission, sir, coming from within the craft."

"The crew? They probably want to say something momentous before blasting off."

"No, sir. It's from the ship itself. I can't pinpoint it exactly; one of the modules whose function we couldn't be sure of."

That doesn't really help, thought the Professor. In truth, they weren't sure of the function of most of the modules.

The Vice President-elect stepped up behind him. "Stop this. Immediately."

"Just a simple transmission," said the Professor. "Maybe something to tell them we are on our way." He turned to the radio operator. "Decipher it. What does it say?"

"I don't know, sir. It doesn't appear to be in the same language that they've used for all the instructions. It might take some time to decipher it."

"Get on it, right away. How much time until lift-off?"

"About fifteen minutes."

"I said, stop this!" said Stanley. He tried to step closer to Grayson but two marines intervened.

"I'm afraid I can't," said Grayson, now slightly nervous. "Even if I wanted to. We thought there might be some issues with the new administration so we removed the abort option after the countdown starts." He smiled weakly and turned to the window again. He checked his watch again. "Not long now," he said to no one in particular, and looked up at the towering starship.

Vice President-elect Stanley came up behind him. "You do know that President Simpson will order it shot down as soon as he is sworn in."

"Unlikely," said the Professor over his shoulder. "There are a dozen American citizens on board."

"What! That was never part of the specification."

"Actually it was, but we decided not to publicize widely. But what would be the point of going to the stars with an unmanned craft? And besides, I doubt that anything in our arsenal could reach it once it takes off. But I suggest you call the President-elect and give him the news. Firing at a starship with American citizens aboard might not go down very well in the opinion polls. You wouldn't want him facing an impeachment hearing on his first day in the job." With that, he turned his back on Stanley and let his gaze travel lovingly up the *Sagan's* full height.

"I will personally see that you rot in jail for the rest of your life!"

Grayson ignored him and continued to stare towards the *Sagan*. "The future begins this very moment," intoned Grayson as he gazed reverentially upward. He glanced at the large digital clock on the wall, which now read 9:59 a.m.. A low rumble emanated from the ship and spread out across the plain. A spurt of flame appeared at its base, and the *Sagan* lifted into the sky.

"Enjoy the show, Senator," Grayson said. The clock on the wall flicked over to 10:00 a.m. as the starship rose higher into the clear morning air. "Or should I say Mr. Vice President."

They both watched the ship rise. But this was not the ponderous never-quite-sure-if-it-will-make-it ascent of a NASA rocket. The *Sagan* sprang upward, giving the moorings barely enough time to drop away. It shot into the clear Montana sky almost faster than their eyes could follow, and was out of human sight in less than twenty seconds. *Christ,* thought the Professor, *I sure hope there is some kind of inertia screen built into the living quarters, or the crew will now be as flat as so many pizzas on the floor. Thin crust pizzas at that.* But he said nothing.

The *Sagan* disappeared from sight, and they turned to the panel of instruments in the control room. All the techs were gathered around one screen where a radar track showed the progress of the spaceship. Grayson pushed his way through the group until he stood behind the screen's operator.

"What's happening?" he asked.

"It's still accelerating, sir. I didn't think anything could pick up speed that quickly. At this rate..." He checked a secondary screen that was filled with numbers. "At this rate, it will reach ninety percent of light speed in less than an hour."

The senator, now officially the Vice President, pushed through the crowd. "Abort it! Now!"

The Professor turned towards him. "I told you, sir, there is no abort," he said softly. Then more firmly, "Besides, why would we abort it? Of course it's accelerating. How else are we going to reach the stars? The only question is whether it will cruise just below light speed or if they have broken that barrier somehow. It may just continue to accelerate..." His voice drifted off and for a moment he let himself imagine the stars, now within reach.

"Sir," said the technician seated at the screen, breaking his reverie again.

Grayson regained his composure and turned back to the screen. "Yes? What's its trajectory? Do you know where it is headed?"

"We're starting to lose it from the satellite trackers sir, but it appears to be headed directly towards the sun."

"Ah," said the Professor. "The old sling-shot maneuver to pick up even more speed. Very clever."

"No sir," said the operator. "It's not in a near-solar trajectory. It is literally headed *directly towards the sun*. At this rate it will impact in less than..."he checked the figures on his secondary screen again "...nineteen minutes."

They all crowded around the screen, craning their heads, staring at the projected flight path on the screen. Everyone in the room watched it in silence for what seemed to be a very long time.

Exactly nineteen minutes later the screen operator turned to the Professor. "No change in the flight path as far as we can tell, sir. I think they will be impacting the sun right now."

Exactly eight minutes later, someone at the back of the crowd noticed a certain brightness filling the room. He tugged the sleeve of the man next to him, and they both turned towards the window where the morning light had brightened as if it were already noon, and then as if it were mid-summer. Soon the entire room had turned away from the screens and towards the window, and they all felt the warmth now flowing through the glass. Snow on the nearby hills was already melting, uncovering the dry winter grasses underneath.

Grayson remembered Ray Bradbury's "Rocket Summer" and thought it was a fitting image for man's first step toward the stars. But the heat continued to pour in through the thick glass window. The sun, still low in the east, began to turn from benign yellow to a bright angry red. Outside the brown grass of the plains erupted into flames.

※※※

153 years later, somewhere in the Hyades cluster, Master M'rapt'ki, second in line to the throne (as befitted his planet's senior scientist), was awakened after midnight by the sound of an ancient alarm.

He called the night shift supervisor, who appeared on his communications screen immediately. "Not a false alarm?" asked M'rapt'ki.

"No sir," replied the night shift supervisor.

"Send me the coordinates."

"Yes sir, right away."

M'rapt'ki glanced at the numbers as they appeared on his screen, then ran up the stairs of the imperial palace to the emperor's sleeping chamber, brushing past the guards with a swift salute. He knocked loudly on the emperor's door and entered without waiting for a reply.

"It's happened, Sire. The interstellar alarm."

The emperor rubbed the sleep from his eye-stalks with his third hand while reaching for his royal robe with his primary. "Are you sure?"

"Yes, Sire. There is no mistake. I have the coordinates here," M'rapt'ki said, gesturing towards his comms device. "I estimate we have about twelve minutes. There should be an excellent view from the balcony."

The emperor dressed quickly and followed his chief scientist through the door and onto the balcony. All three moons had set, and the sky was as dark as it ever was. Which is to say it was a soft grey, given the close proximity of at least a dozen neighboring stars in the cluster, shining brightly in every quarter of the sky.

"There," said M'rapt'ki, pointing to an almost invisible star in the direction of the galactic centre.

"Tell me again, M'rapt'ki, is this really necessary? Will we ever come across a race that we can *communicate* with, rather than simply destroy it?"

"It is the only way we can be certain, Sire. Any species with the wit to understand our signals and to build the device is a potential threat. We must trust no one."

"But the entire solar system as well? Why? Will we ever know if we find a race that is worth preserving?"

"The test is simple, Excellency, and was established scientifically by our evolutionary psychologists long ago. If a race receives our messages but, instead of building and immediately launching the device, takes the trouble to discover its mechanisms, they may indeed be worthy of interacting with ourselves."

High in the northern sky, 153 light years away, a faint yellow star began to glow ever more brightly.

End of Days

Daniel M. Kimmel

No one thought the end of the world would be like this. After decades of divisiveness, sectarianism, nationalism, partisanship, holy wars, secular wars, and one crisis after another, people were burnt out. They just wanted to be left alone no matter what the new alleged "crisis" of the hour was. A takeover of the Earth by alien overlords from Alpha Centauri? Most people couldn't be troubled to pay much attention.

Phil and Sam were sitting at the NCO club nursing their beers when the TV blurted out, "We interrupt our regularly scheduled programming for this emergency message from the President of the United States. President...um, Smith, will be addressing the nation from that round office. The Oval Office, that's it. Ladies and gentlemen, President Smith."

Phil was already facing the TV. Sam tried to decide if it was worth turning around but then he realized he could see a reflection of one of the TV screens in the mirror behind the bar and sat where he was. He'd hear everything just the same.

"My fellow Americans, a short while ago we received the following message from a creature identifying itself as Grand General Braxis, Commander of the Earth Occupation."

The image flickered and was replaced by the image of a hideous monster, its head surrounded by long, oily, blue hair, and three waving tentacles. It spoke from a mouth situated over its two eyes. "People of Earth," he/she/it declared, "you are now under the subjugation of the Alpha Centauri Expeditionary Force. All will kneel before the might and power of our beloved Imperial Ruler Groflax. You now live and serve at his whim. Be warned that resistance will be met with the fiercest possible measures..."

The Grand General was cut off in midsentence and the screen returned to a live image of President Smith. "I am reporting to you that after full consideration with my top advisors, we have responded with the following statement: 'So what?'" With that he leaned back in his chair. "And thank you for listening."

The image faded out as an announcer's voice declared, "We now return you to our regularly scheduled programming."

On screen—in mid-episode—was "Garbage Pickers," the hit reality show in which contestants picked through mounds of trash in hopes of finding a single diamond worth a reported one million dollars. It had been the number one show for the last three years, even though—or perhaps because—no one had yet found the diamond.

Phil turned to Sam reflexively, before he even had time to wonder if making eye contact with his fellow noncom was worth the effort. "Sounds serious. Think we ought to report in?"

"Why bother? They know where to find us if they need something," answered Sam.

Around the base, indeed, around the nation, business went on as usual, which was to say very little business took place at all. People were mildly curious how this new crisis might play out, if only as a distraction from their day-to-day lives, but no one seemed to think it would actually change anything.

Forty-eight hours later, without warning, the Alpha Centauri fleet showed they meant business by destroying four of the five boroughs of New York City. In what was taken to be an act of whimsy, they had spared Staten Island.

With no new orders to interrupt their day, Phil and Sam spent their free time at the NCO club, sipping their beers and occasionally paying attention to the news.

"Bummer about New York, Sam."

"Really? You have family there?"

"No, but I have leave next month and I finally got tickets to see 'Hamilton.' Guess that won't be happening now."

In the days to come, similar attacks were carried out on London, Paris, Moscow, Beijing and Mumbai, and yet the world continued to turn. It wasn't as though they hadn't seen it all before in dozens of movies. So now it was on their TV screens instead of in their movie theaters. It still had all the trappings of run of the mill entertainment. Of course, the people in those cities might have been a tad upset, but they were all dead and consequently their opinions carried very little weight.

Despite the carnage, life went on as if nothing had changed. Sure enough, exactly as if Earth had united in creating a mighty force to defend the home planet, the attacks ceased. That nothing had been required of humanity simply demonstrated that waiting them out had been the right strategy. For two weeks, nothing further happened, and online discussions returned to the normal chatter about cute animals and people exchanging photographs of their meals.

It was then that what were described as alien tankers appeared at several spots around the Earth's equator. They were huge beyond imagining and, for people living on equatorial land within hundreds of miles of the ships, it was like a permanent eclipse. No one was quite sure what this was about, but then the ships began drawing millions of gallons of water from the oceans, pumping the water up to the tankers in an around the clock operation. As during past global crises, the world turned to America for leadership. A week after the pumping began, President Smith finally addressed the global community.

After recapitulating what everyone already knew, he paused, and then smiled. "And thus I'm happy to report that the debate over climate change is over. We had been warned that if we did nothing, the melting of the polar ice caps would cause sea levels to rise, flooding our coastal cities. Now, thanks to Alpha Centauri, the excess water has been drained off, and our cities are safe. So, let's get back to what we were doing."

By the next morning the ships had all withdrawn. Instead, small ships now began to land in the Pacific Northwest. A decree by Grand General Braxis declared that all residents from age 5 and up in the states of Washington, Oregon, and Idaho would now be engaged in forced service— what some were calling "slavery"—to extract natural resources from mines and forests for use by the alien forces. Instead of decrying this action as inhumane, unconstitutional, cruel, or dozens of other words that had fallen into neglect except by those who treasured their thesauruses, the story was reported—when it was reported at all—as indicating a major drop in the unemployment rate, and proof that the government's economic policies were bearing fruit.

At the NCO club, Phil and Sam were nursing their beers and Sam was looking for the waitress to order another round. She was standing under the "No Smoking" sign enjoying a cigarette.

"Miss? Can we get two more beers?"

"I'm on break," she snapped back, "You want another round, get it yourself." Without complaint, Phil and Sam went behind the bar and refilled their glasses.

"Put it on our tab," said Phil.

"Whatever," said the waitress, who headed back into the kitchen.

On the screen over the bar, an image appeared indicating "Breaking News." Sam grabbed for the remote and switched channels. There were similar bulletins everywhere else, including the sports and cooking channels.

"Must be important," Sam muttered, putting down the remote and rejoining Phil at their table.

On the TV, a man was manacled to a chair as Grand General Braxis faced the camera. "People of Earth," it began, "we warned you that your puny forces could not possibly triumph over the might of Alpha Centauri. To demonstrate this, we have captured the leader of the Resistance and will force you to watch as he is tortured into confessing his crimes and naming his associates. *This*," he emphasized, "is the fate of those who dare to oppose us."

With that, Braxis took one of his tentacles and wrapped it around the throat of the human.

"Isn't that Harvey?" asked Phil.

"Harvey who?"

"I don't know his last name. The guy from 'Garbage Pickers.'"

On screen Braxis demanded, "What is your name, puny human?"

"Harvey," replied the man in the chair. "And would you mind not doing that? It hurts."

"I told you it was Harvey," said Phil, as he rose to top up his beer again.

Braxis took a second tentacle and lifted Harvey's head so that they made eye contact. "It is *supposed* to hurt. Now, Harvey, are you ready to confess to your crimes?"

Harvey's blank expression didn't change. "What crimes?"

"Leading the Resistance, sabotage, disseminating propaganda against the Alpha Centauri state..."

"Whoa, man," said Harvey, showing the most signs of life yet, "I don't know what you're talking about. I just pick through garbage looking for the diamond. Gonna find it, too."

"I'm not interested in your human rituals," roared Braxis. "Give me the names of the other leaders of the Resistance."

"The Resistance? What's that?"

"The people disrupting our occupation of Earth. Don't bother to deny it."

Harvey returned to his blank stare. "Deny it? I don't even know what you're talking about."

Braxis thumped Harvey on the head with his third tentacle. "Are you claiming not to be aware that we have laid waste to your cities, stolen your resources and enslaved your people?"

Sam turned to Phil. "How come it's picking on the little guy? He should pick on someone his own size."

Phil burped. "Is there anyone his?"

"I don't know," replied Sam. "You think maybe this is like a bonus round of the game? Maybe Harvey found the diamond."

"Don't think so," said Phil. "They would have showed it."

Braxis released his grip on Harvey and started oozing around the room, going back and forth in front of the camera. Finally, he turned to the viewing audience. "What is the matter with you humans? The whole point of conquering a planet is subjugating the indigent population with our superior technology and ruthless exploitation. If you just sit there and take it, where's the fun in that?"

Braxis started pacing again. Behind him, Harvey was trying to get out of the chair but the manacles wouldn't allow him to do so. "Could someone please take these off? I need to get back to the dump."

"Garbage. Do you believe it? He's talking about garbage." Braxis swung in Harvey's direction. "Suppose I told you I was going to destroy Kansas City if you didn't immediately give me the names of the ringleaders of the Resistance?"

Harvey seemed to ponder this for a moment. Then he looked at Braxis. "Always wanted to go to Kansas City."

"What!" screamed the Grand General.

"Heard you could get really good steak there."

"I can't take it anymore. You slugs are the laziest, the stupidest, the most apathetic..."

"Hey, man."

With that, Braxis started tearing through the room, smashing things. As he turned towards Harvey, a squad of several Alpha Centauri soldiers rushed in and grabbed Braxis. As they scuffled, the camera swung wildly until the image was replaced with that of a man picking through garbage. "I found it," he shouted and brushed off his find, only to power down. "Never mind. It was a salt shaker."

"I think this is a rerun," said Sam.

"How can you tell?"

"Well, isn't that Harvey?"

"I think you're right."

The next afternoon, there was a brief announcement from an unidentified member of the Alpha Centauri high command declaring that the occupation was over and that they were unilaterally withdrawing, admitting defeat against Earth's cruel and unprecedented use of psychological warfare. By nightfall, the ships were all gone from the Earth's surface and surrounding orbits.

Phil and Sam celebrated their victory over the Alpha Centauri Expeditionary Forces by having a beer at the NCO club.

"Sure wish I could have seen some of that psychological warfare," said Phil. "It must have really been something."

"I'll bet," agreed Sam. "It would be nice to have something going on, wouldn't it?"

That's Not My Apocalypse...

Liam Hogan

Tick, tock.

The hands of the Doomsday clock stand once again at two minutes to midnight. So join me as I countdown to the end of human existence and find out what lurks behind that twelfth, and very final, chime.

Welcome, to *That's Not My Apocalypse!*

10--Nuclear Armageddon

I grew up under the scintillating shadow of a mushroom cloud, spent my formative years with Mutual Assured Destruction the definitive, end-of-the-world scenario. The atom bomb is the ultimate weapon of mass destruction, so feared that the people who invented it, created the Doomsday Clock to make sure everyone *else* couldn't sleep at night. The Clock first marked two minutes to Armageddon back in 1953, with *New! Improved!* hydrogen bombs. For decades, it's tracked global tensions, burgeoning nuclear arsenals, and the odd test ban treaty, yo-yoing between Twelve! Whole! Minutes! and not long enough to boil an egg.

It wasn't to last. The end of my youth also saw the end of the Soviet Union. The expanded nuclear club banded together to stop anyone else joining the fun, the US eased back on the hair trigger, and the Cold War was over. By 1991, the Clock stood at seventeen minutes.

The club *does* keep growing, with North Korea the latest party crasher. And world leaders tweeting: "I've got more nukes than you", doesn't exactly help. No surprise then that those seventeen minutes half-lifed away. A nuke is still a nuke whether it's an "active deterrent", stockpiled, or dismantled, and there are plenty left to do the job an unhealthy number of times over.

The hands of the Doomsday Clock will always glow in the dark and nukes may haunt our disaster movies and apocalyptic novels, but:

Nuclear Armageddon?

That's not my apocalypse. Its rhetoric is too 1950's. (60s, 70s, 80s...).

9--Asteroid Impact

I'm looking up, to see the next thing that brings us down.

Asteroids are the *ultimate* extinction event. Been there, done that, will merrily do so again. But when?

Reassuringly, not any time soon. NASA's Near Earth Object program tracks twenty thousand NEOs, of which fewer than two thousand are PHA's: Potentially Hazardous Asteroids. The bigger the hazard, the easier it is to keep tabs on. Perhaps too easy. From tabloid headlines of so called "close" passes, you'd think there was barely room between the earth and the moon to reverse park a small rock. The moon is sixty earth radii away: if it orbited the edges of a dart board, the earth would fit comfortably within the bullseye.

True, the bullseye *does* get hit by a hundred tons of space material every day—pass a strong magnet along the sludge in your gutter and collect some space dust! But we only have to worry about the *big* chunks. The bolide that flattened trees around Tunguska, Siberia in 1908 was tiny, merely 45m across. A hundred-meter asteroid impacts every ten thousand years, but this would only cause a *local* apocalypse. We can expect a mile-wide asteroid every hundred thousand years, and a potential dinosaur eliminating, six-mile monster—equivalent to a billion Hiroshimas—once every hundred million years.

What we would do if we spotted a Torino scale 9 or 10 object is a moot point: Bruce Willis may or may not be available. But NASA isn't tracking anything that poses even a moderate risk in my lifetime.

Before you get too complacent, statistics should still make you nervously watch the skies. An impact event may be unlikely, but the body count would be very, very high. The dinosaurs would concur, if...well. Y'know. (Too soon?)

Asteroid impact?
That's not my apocalypse. Its odds are too astronomically low.

8--Zombies

Seriously? You know they're fictional, right? Moving screamingly along...

7--Gamma Ray Burster

A gamma ray burster is the focused, energetic death of a pair of neutron stars or black holes. As the super-massive duo tango to their doom, a virulent beam of cosmic rays are released along the axis of rotation. GRBs are the biggest bang since the big one; a million trillion times brighter than the sun.

So powerful that if one happened within, say, a hundred light years and was pointed our way, it would strip the earth's fragile ozone layer. A GRB is *possibly* implicated in a major extinction event half a billion years ago, but as yet, nobody has claimed responsibility.

Here's the kicker: our end may already have happened. That's light years for you. And other than cowering beneath a very large rock, there's absolutely nothing we can do.

Gamma Ray Burster?
That's not my apocalypse. Its death is too uncaring.

6--Alien Invasion

Aliens aren't real. Not ones that traverse interstellar distances at faster than light speeds to threaten our cows, our water supplies, or our Lieutenant Ripleys.

Assuming they don't come from Mars.

5--Global Warming

When you get around to asking why the Doomsday Clock stands once again at two minutes to midnight, the short answer is global warming.

Even if you're a denier, it's still the answer. The relation between CO_2 and atmospheric temperature was established over fifty years ago, itself the result of work done, and largely forgotten until given a male face, by Eunice Foote, in 1856.

Of all the apocalyptic scenarios, *this* one has already begun. Twenty of the warmest years on record have been in the last twenty-two years, CO_2 is 50% above pre-industrial levels, and global temperatures are up one degree Celsius. Uncertainty and complexity in climate modelling are not whether it will get hotter if we pump more greenhouse gases into the atmosphere (duh!), but whether there are tipping points along the way that will make the situation even worse, such as methane unlocked from beneath a defrosting tundra, or the refusal of the oceans to soak up any more excess heat and CO_2. These increased but uncertain risks are hardly excuses oil and gas industries can fall back on because the "science is unclear".

While the polar bears may be doomed (sorry, polar bears), surely we wouldn't be so stupid as to cause a seventh great extinction event? Surely we can limit warming to one and a half degrees? Surely, by now, we've managed to cap our carbon emissions?

No? Oh.

Nobody said it was going to be easy. And, with every uptick in parts per million, the problem we eventually have to solve gets more difficult.

Capitalism and global warming are so closely entwined that a world in which we are encouraged *not* to consume is going to require pretty radical change. But it doesn't *feel* like an apocalypse yet.

Perhaps that's why so little has been done. Because the lovely people who brought you this apocalypse, and the aging politicians dragging their feet, and ok, yes, me, will all be dead before the worst of it hits. And old people do suffer so from the cold.

Global Warming?

That's not my apocalypse. That's my kids' apocalypse (sorry, kids).

4--Bad Science

Physicists have nightmares just as terrible as astronomers. One of their more peculiar nocturnal fears is that the laws of the universe aren't fixed. If our solar system were to wander into a section of the cosmos where the strong, weak, or electromagnetic forces varied by even the tiniest amount, it would upset the delicate balance that holds atoms together, that keep neutrons neutrons, that allow electrons to orbit where they need to for the many wonderful chemical reactions that sustain life.

Physicists propose this scenario to explain away the unexplainable, like dark matter. If the maths doesn't work, (they suggest), maybe it's because it doesn't apply everywhere.

If true, the laws would also change over time. Physicists have a tool capable of measuring such infinitesimal differences: an interferometer. This detects shifts of "half a wiggle". LIGO, for instance, detects half a wiggle of laser light over five kilometres, making it sensitive to gravity ripples from the death-duet of twin black holes, millions of light years away.

Similar tests put limits on just how unstable the laws of physics are. And, as far as we can tell, they're incredibly stable.

Phew!

Bad Science?
That's not my apocalypse. Its theories are too theoretical.

3--Supervolcanoes

If you were travelling in the time of the dinosaurs, you'd need a set of maps for the supercontinent, *Pangaea*. And geologists predict the continental plates will come back together again in 250 million years to form *Pangaea Ultima*.

The thin crust we live on sometimes develops an angry boil. Supervolcano eruptions are capable of ejecting a thousand cubic kilometres of magma.

While the localised effects would be terrible, it's the consequences for the atmosphere that makes these potential end-gamers. Releasing a potent brew of greenhouse gases and sunlight-blocking aerosols, they would plunge the earth into a decade-long winter. 1816's Year Without a Summer was a sniffle by comparison.

Some supervolcanoes—including Yellowstone—have their own doomsday clocks: magma chambers that fill and then empty with a degree of regularity. Yellowstone erupted 2.1 million, 1.3 million, and 640,000 years ago. I guess it's about due.

There are also ominous signs in the Campi Flegrei ("burning fields") in Italy, a supervolcano that plunged temperatures in Europe by as much as 4C, 39,000 years ago, and may have contributed to the demise of the Neanderthals. Another, Toba in Indonesia, is sometimes cited as the cause of mankind's "genetic bottleneck" 75,000 years ago, though recent archaeological evidence suggests otherwise.

But hey, none of these supervolcanoes are grumbling *quite* enough to worry about.

Supervolcano?
That's not my apocalypse. Its magma chamber is too empty.

2--Population Pressure

There's an irony in suggesting our ultimate downfall might be because we, as a species, are *too* successful.

The population of the earth has more than doubled in my lifetime. The growth rate is falling, particularly where wealth is concentrated, but the global population continues to rise.

There is no planet B, climate protesters protest, and even if there were, we'd fill it within a generation. More significant than head count is the growth in demand for resources. We are the privileged few, and we can't, and shouldn't, stop others attaining the same quality of life we enjoy. But if that level is at today's (US) level, we're going to need another five earths—planets B, C, D, E *AND* F. And never mind dire predictions of the future; we're already using one and a half earths based on carbon emissions.

Malthus wasn't *wrong*, per se, even if the dates for societal collapse drift by like deadlines for the Rapture. Because if our population and consumption keep growing then at some point Malthus will be able to turn in his overcrowded grave and say: See? I *TOLD* you so.

Anyone for Soylent Green?

Population Pressure?

That's not my apocalypse. Its predictions are too Malthusian.

1--Global Pandemic

A glut of humans is an opportunity just begging to be exploited. Not for zombies or aliens, but for the most successful family of life on earth: bacteria.

We forget how deadly disease has been through most of human history. We forget that wounds fester, that childhood was once such a minefield of contagion you were lucky to reach adulthood, and that the reason cancer is such a major killer is because other things *aren't*.

Smallpox paved the way for the conquering of the Americas, setting down a marker for the start of the Anthropocene: the *lowering* of CO_2 levels as farmed land returned to the wild.

Black Death rolled across Europe in waves between the 14th and 17th century, killing between 30% and 60% of the population, having taken a breather after polishing off the Roman Empire a millennium earlier. And plague isn't just a horror from medieval times; it put in a brief appearance in San Francisco as recent as the turn of the twentieth century.

We have tamed many ills, but it would be presumptuous to believe them gone forever. Deadly bacteria are always lurking in the wings, waiting for another opportunity. If not cholera, typhus or tuberculosis, then something we haven't seen before, something the World Health Organization call: "Disease X".

Perhaps it will be less exotic than that. The 1918 outbreak of H1N1 influenza infected one *third* of the world's population, killing fifty million—more than all the bullets and the bombs of WW1. Bird flu, H5N1, has a mortality rate of 60%. And H1N1 hasn't gone away, returning most recently as swine flu.

That influenza subtypes are named after animals highlights one of the problems. Viruses and microbes evolve and don't need humans overdosing on antibiotics to do so. Cats, dogs, pigs, birds, bats...even whales get the flu. Though catching flu from a whale is probably tricky.

There are over a hundred subtypes of influenza, only a handful of which are highly contagious and this doesn't include H5N1. Not *yet*.

Humans aren't exactly a mono-crop like the Cavendish banana, but we do have relatively low nucleotide diversity. When a new killer disease hits, we're *all* susceptible. And with air travel, we're all going to be exposed, pretty damned quick.

Fortunately, the deadliest diseases tend to burn themselves out. Dead hosts (zombies excepting) don't usually spread disease (Ebola excepting).

But maybe it doesn't have to be that deadly. What percentage mortality *is* an apocalypse, anyway?

Modern infrastructure is fragile and becoming more so as Just-In-Time AI's attempt to minimise waste—to save money, not the planet. If disease decimated the healthcare system, closed the schools, prevented travel, stopped deliveries, brought industry to a standstill... how long would our societies survive? How many hot meals away are we from anarchy?

We live blessed lives, regardless of what alternative truths rose-tinted nostalgia tell us. We live in a time of plenty, of relative peace, of astonishing technological advances that our children take for granted. Which is as it should be. Progress *is* lovely.

And really, I don't *want* it all to end. But Cormac McCarthy's *The Road* teaches me it's best to go out in the first wave of any *truly* awful disaster.

So don't be surprised, as death rides in on a pale horse, to find me over at the nearest quarantine centre, unmasked, breathing deeply.

Global pandemic?
That's my apocalypse! Its R_0 is *so* infectious!

The END (of the world...?)

Alternative Apocalypse

Sitting Here in Limbo

Mikal Trimm

End Of The World for you?

Yeah, me too. Didn't figure you for one of those End Of The Line wanks. Too easy, right? Go out alone? No style.

What'd you go for? *Nuclear Winter*, no shit? Heard that one takes a long time, man. Well, you know, subjectively, anyway. I went for *The Cataclysm* myself. Nothing like a giant asteroid hitting the Earth to give you that sense of the inevitable.

Had a friend who went for *Judgment Day*. You know, with the saints taken up, and the thousand-year reign and crap. I hear that's the longest program they have, really depressing, beat-yourself-to-death-with-guilt scenario. Who needs that garbage, right? 'Course, Rick had *issues*, know what I mean? Maybe he got off on it, I dunno.

My old man went the easy route back when they started this whole gig. He took one of the first *End Of The Line* scenarios they came out with—killed in a shoot-out with the cops, I think. Mom told me she didn't even know about it until the bill came. He was supposed to get her signature or something, but he faked it somehow. This was back before they got their act together and put in all the safeguards, I guess.

Hey, if you're doing the *Nuclear Winter* gig, I guess you had to get all the memory implants, right? So that you get the whole package at the end? Damn, I hear there's a pretty good wait for all that stuff. You must really be serious about this. I just want to lie down, let the asteroid blow me to smithereens, and be done with it, y'know?

Why? I dunno, son of a suicide, all that jazz. Yeah, that's kind of a cop-out, I guess. Hah! Cop-out! My old man would've liked that one. I can see him now: "Come an' get me, ya lousy pigs!" Hail of bullets... Not bad, Pop, not bad at all. You were a pretty tough old bastard, now that I think about it.

Guess I'm just tired of all the crap out there, to be honest. World's full of it, people are full of it, hell, *I'm* full of it. I just want out.

Of course, I don't mind the idea of taking everyone else with me either, right? I consider this "suicide on a grand scale". Don't know where I heard that, but I always liked the line.

Well, that's my name they're calling. Time to visit Dreamland, buddy. Should be one *helluva* dream.

Hey, pal. See ya on the other side...

A Pebble in the Data Stream

Michelle F Goddard

The Tunnel is closed. I am as far from home as I have ever been, separated by stone and barbed wire and grounded surveillance drones that nap on the cold earth. I shiver and pace the narrow width between the service tube walls. Cold rolls up fear in my belly like tar.

I push back my sleeve and check my watch. I follow the second hand as it slips its way around. The whir of wound gears jitters on my skin; springs and coils, springs and coils. I rub my thumb against my writer's callus, that fleshy pad on the middle finger earned word by word and page by page as I wait for the window of opportunity to open and for me to find the courage to move.

"No. Don't let her near it," someone said.

Called to the front of the classroom, I stood beside the computer terminal, but not touching it, as glares poked me harder than knobby fingers. Sweat sprung up on the nape of my neck. I heard their taunt riding the back of their teeth. With a hissing squeal that dipped down to a guttural drone, the screen went blank and doomed my fate.

"Jinx," someone said, as fingers snapped and hoots erupted. "Alasie jinxed it out."

"Calm down," Teacher said. "It's just a technical glitch." A real teacher. No virtual prof, but flesh. Usually someone's parent or older sibling back from trying their fortune in the city. Still, Teacher, capital "T". She bent down to jiggle the power cable. "You can go back to your seat, Alasie."

I slunk to my desk at the back of the classroom. Grey light from outside drifted through the classroom windows, filtered by sparse scrub and spare trees that stood scattered throughout the commons. In the centre stood the town, our vertical village, a single condo tower grey and stern as the sky. From this hub, tunnels connected the outlying buildings including the community centre and our school, but everything else—homes, businesses, even stores—were all housed inside the condo.

I opened my workbook, rubbing my callus as I worked through the questions printed out especially for me. Jack sat beside me, his fingers flying across a tablet hidden under the desk, his gaze flitting from the room then back to the screen. His hungry intensity drew me. My curiosity reached out to touch him too sharply.

"Mind your business," Jack said with a scowl.

"Mind your own," I said, voice like a slap. The ceiling lights went out. Cries of shock and glee pierced the dark.

"I suppose that is all for today," the teacher said, as shoes squeaked against the linoleum as they moved toward the door.

Tablet screens flickered through the corridor toward the tower entrance, emergency lights dyeing sneakers yellow. The sound of clapping doors punctuated the wave of shuffling feet, as students poured into the condo tower of The Enclave; a nicer name for our neighbourhood than it deserves.

After the Reconstruction, they gathered us into Enclaves, repurposed military outposts, to live and work, side by side, one on top of the other. Those a little better off lived a little higher up, but not much. No one has much. Anyone with much would live in the city: those mushroom clusters of silver towers strung together by cobweb silk highways and veiled in shimmering clouds. Streams of light seemed to flow so easily out there, but choked up once they got to the Enclave. But I suspected that how far away we lived didn't account for all the power fluctuations.

The hallway lights flared back to life by the time I had pushed through the main doors, but the other students had made their escape and there was no re-jailing them. I descended to the ground floor and my uncle's workshop attached to the machinery stables. "Uncle Niimi," I said. "Uncle. There was a blackout."

Maggie ducked her head out of her workshop. She saw me, smiled and crept out until she stood pressed against the doorway as if it needed her help to stay upright.

"Where's Uncle Niimi, Maggie?"

Maggie Magpie, my uncle's helper, another bird like me, fallen from a nest and saved by my uncle, shrugged and held out something that looked like a glove. "Working. See?"

"Yes. But where's Uncle."

"Working. Working," Maggie said, and turned around, her straight black braids whipping out to slap the door frame before she disappeared back into her workroom. She was already seated, slouched over her project lying on the workbench when I passed by. I smelt solder and tasted bitter metal in my mouth and moved on toward the backroom. I found Uncle Niimi slouched in his chair, pale and sweating.

"Maggie!" At my call, I heard her galloping shuffle skid to a stop. "Get water."

Uncle's head lolled on his shoulders but he blinked and sipped as I held the glass to his lips. Maggie hovered so close I could hardly breathe. "Now, you're worried?" I said. "You're useless."

"Alasie, nothing is useless," Uncle Niimi said, as Maggie, all hanging head and wringing hands, backed away. "Everything has its purpose."

Darkness bears down on me. I crouch; arms wrapped around one knee while the other presses against concrete. I glance behind. I see the suggestion of night at the entrance but turn away. My flashlight leaks a washed-out beam onto the damp ground. The walls, grey and pitted, are painted with drips of dark moisture. Cold iron bars stand before me. The panel is just on the other side, blinking lights all green and cheerful. But green is not for go. Not yet. I glance at my watch, pull my coat tighter around me and pat the gloves tucked into my pocket.

The healer came. Her eyes uttered warnings into the hush as her hands moved to Uncle Niimi's forehead and neck. She bent low to whisper. Uncle Niimi nodded before she brought the quilt up to his chin. Afterward, I stood in the

163

doorway, and glared up at her as the lights of our apartment flickered.

"I've done what I can. Your uncle needs city medicine. Remind him to contact the med-boards."

The green lights of the panel flicker and dim. The time is now. I inhale sharply and affix the phalanx, a segmented rod with a harness that fits around my wrist onto the end of my index finger. Praying the end will reach, I extend the pointer. I hold it up to the light as I run my hand along its length. This is more than a test of this new tool. This is a test of faith. Am I brave enough? Is he as smart as he thinks he is?

Sliding my hand through the bars, I stab in the code, my finger quivering with fear between each jab. I retract the phalanx. The panel goes dark as the bars click and release the lock. I slide past the heavy metal gate, shutting it firmly behind me. Shutting me in. The panel flickers to life and resumes its lazy blinking. I march down the corridor, my boots slapping against the ground like the tick of a clock.

Just after dinner, Jack showed up at our door. It wasn't unusual for someone to show up looking to have something repaired, or a piece of tech scavenged or salvaged. But Jack had never visited.

He shoved his tablet at me and scowled. "Get this fixed, jinx."

I stood, arms folded and shoulders hunched like a cornered cat.

"What is this?" Uncle Niimi said, still haggard, fisting sleep from his eyes as he trudged to the door, shrugging deeper into the blanket wrapped around his shoulders.

"This is her fault," Jack said. Again, he thrust the tablet at me like a knife, like unwanted news, like truth.

I looked down to find it flashing and humming in my hand. The screen warmed and welcomed me.

"What did you do?" Jack said.

"Nothing," I said and shoved the tablet into his belly.

Jack swiped the screen, releasing the keyboard. "You've bypassed my security."

"Goodnight, Jack," Uncle Niimi said, and shuffled back to bed, pulling his blanket tighter around his shoulders against a cold that wasn't in the room.

Jack didn't move from the doorway, but watched Uncle Niimi disappear into his room. "What's wrong with him?"

"Mind your business," I said.

Jack leaned toward me. "I thought you only messed up tech but that's not all, is it." He stared down at his tablet. "I could use your help."

"Why should I?"

"Could earn some change. A bit of coin in your pocket?"

I scanned Jack and didn't like the specs. "No."

I jog along the corridor, and scan the ceiling, noting the stilled cameras attached every few paces, winking red eye shut and blind. Their disability will not be noticed during the maintenance, if he parsed the data correctly. I slip on my gloves and reach behind to touch the quiet neuro-link against the skin at the base of my skull. My body needs only the slightest excuse to shuck it, so I must stay calm. With my other hand, I pat my jacket and feel for the thin rectangle of his jump drive; a pebble in my pocket.

Earlier, Uncle Niimi had waved away my reminder to contact the med-boards as if it were a bothersome crow. His dismissal had disturbed me. Almost as much as Jack's stares that pressed on me and made it hard to breathe.

"How's your uncle?" Jack asked. "Did he get in contact with the med-boards?"

"How did you...?"

Jack smirked. I wanted to rip his lips off.

"Want to know what they said?"

I couldn't help myself. My body leaned toward him and my gaze slid to his tablet. I saw my uncle's name followed by a long list of words that seemed in another language, then numbers and percentages and a single-word tally. Rejected. "That isn't real."

"You wanna bet? Was an easy hack." He smirked and shrugged. "Data-hoarders screwed you over."

"What?"

Jack rolled his eyes, which only made me want to gouge them out.

"They fish the internet and gather all the information on you. Crunch it, filter it down and sell it. Can tell what you want. What you're gonna want. The stream shows how the money flows."

"How?"

"Predictive Algorithms. Where do you think all those forms you fill out end up? Well, maybe not you, but regular folk. It takes all the information collected about you, all the information you feed it, gobbles it up, and spits you out. Marketing-cons. Money-seers. Med-boards are all about them too."

"And because of that, Uncle Niimi can't get medical aid?"

Jack nodded.

"Can you change that?"

Jack leaned back in his chair, arms folded, smug as sunrise.

I hear the soft whir of a camera rotating and focusing its lens. I press myself against the wall and turn off my light. I tug my hood lower around my face. Did I trip an alarm? Is it motion activated?

The camera stops. I stare into the darkness almost daring it to move again. I take in two quick breaths as I slip one hand out of a glove. Hugging the shadows, I slide forward keeping my face down. The camera mount shifts in its socket. Searching? Running my hand along the wall, I reach for a tingle to trace the tech. I slide my finger along it and send out a pulse. The whir of the camera dips to nothing and the lens sags to face the ground.

The tablets littering my bed winked off and on. Each powered up to the factory default screen, yet all the files and folders lay open on the desktop. I let go of my breath and wiped the sweat from the back of my neck. I lay back on my bed as the ache at my temples throbbed.

"What are you doing?" Uncle Niimi asked, standing in the doorway.

"Nothing," I said, covertly sliding my blanket over the tablets.

Uncle Niimi glared at them. "Whose are these?"

"Jack's."

"All of these?"

"They're nothing. Junk. Garbage."

"Alasie, I don't want you hanging out with Jack."

"What? Why?"

"His stats read all wrong. He's trouble. He'll get you in trouble. Get rid of this."

"You have tech you work on. That you scavenge—"

"Enough, Alasie. I came in here to give you these." Uncle Niimi pulled out a pair of gloves, fine mesh and smooth polymer so flimsy they wafted in the paltry breeze. "Maggie made these for you. For when you work on the computers. Maybe you won't have your..." He hesitated. "Troubles."

I slipped on the gloves, the fine threads of the alloy catching on my callus. The gloves were soft and pliable, but seemed durable. I dragged one tablet closer, swiped it to the homepage and pulled up the virtual keyboard and a fresh document. I began to type and marvelled that there was not one flicker or glitch.

I glanced over the edge of the tablet to where Uncle Niimi leaned against the doorway, his breath a labour. "Did you contact the med-boards?"

"I've got my appointment all lined up."

I didn't have Jack's skills to infiltrate the data and see for myself. But I trusted what he said more than my Uncle's shifting gaze. More than the cough he tried to swallow and hide behind his hastily turned back and raised hand.

A few more steps in the dark. In the silence. I turn on my flashlight and glance at my watch. My caution cost me time. I see the door ahead. I run, my hand reaching out, my body feeling the surge build. I press my hand near the handle of the door and grunt as I let my nerves loose in a focused pulse. I hear a click. The door opens.

I bundled Jack's tech into a bag and slogged them up to his apartment. I released them at his feet. "There. I've done what you told me. Now. Set an appointment for my uncle."

"I can't."

My hands closed into fists. "But that's the deal." I felt heat rise up from my core. My skin shimmered as light rippled from me. The power died; the fridge chugged down, the hum of the heating whispered out, the digital readouts faded. The lights in the corridor winked out one at a time. The hall sank into darkness, eaten up by silence.

"You idiot," Jack said, pulling me inside and slamming his front door shut.

Beyond the door lies the server room, a small installation for the outlying areas; an insignificant hub, a nothing node for those riding the edge of the grid. The floor tiles however, are white and spotless. I remove my muddy boots and slip them into the plastic bag wadded into my pocket. The row of servers reminds me of home. The lights along its surface twinkle like the condo windows, our lives framed in each square. Each panel a door into a universe.

I swing the shoe bag onto my back as I slide my foot across the floor. I stand at the terminal, insert the jump drive and reboot the system. The screen goes black and then green as he said it would. Lines of white code flow across the display and the page scrolls down. Then it stops. The code pulses. It turns red. My heart jumps into my throat as a bell chimes far too insistently to be anything but an alarm.

A half an hour later, the black-out still gripped the tower in its fist. Most of the Enclave had emptied into the commons. Concern and curiosity coloured their grumbles until they were as dark as the tower. The grey block of glass and concrete gone cold and dead had not a light in one window. Outside in the courtyard, technicians—tools in hand—ran to the machinery stables to check the power grid.

Jack appeared beside me. "Hurry." He grabbed my hand and dragged me toward the scraggily-brambled field that surrounded the town. He pointed to a spot just above the horizon. "They sent a surveillance drone to check out the blackout." The drone skimmed the contour of the rocky ground growing larger as it sailed toward us. "You've got to disable it."

Panic ran through me like electricity. It felt enough to power the Enclave. "How?"

"Figure it out, Alasie, because if you don't, they'll zero-in on you as the disruptor."

I focused my mind on the flying drone, reaching out to touch it, through the metallic shell, past the wires and into the aether at its core, winding it down until it lay tame on the ground.

The pinging increases in tempo. My heart beats so hard I can barely breathe. I am grateful for my gloves, otherwise I would have shorted out the entire system. I press my gloved index and middle finger to the neuro-link making sure it has full contact. I breathe in through my nose and out through my mouth. "Jack," I say, hating the quiver in my voice. "Jack. There's an alarm beeping on the computer."

"No big." I can practically hear his shrug, his annoying, smug, shrug. So easy to shrug from his safe distance, in the silence of his no-alarm-pinging bunker. "You have to ghost through to reset the temporary password."

"What password."

"Just use password. That's not too hard is it?"

The morning after the black-out, officials came rolling through the tunnel. The two uniformed investigators marched through the main entrance of the Enclave scanning the area with snooping eyes that no one could meet with a steady gaze. Hope lived briefly when they asked to see my uncle, but they saw him at the machinery stables not our apartment.

Uncle Niimi leaned against his counter, a counter clear of clutter. Unusual, but not because of the visitors. He was too sick to work.

"It looks clean enough," one official said to the other, lowering his scanner. They nodded and turned to leave.

"Is that it?" I asked. "My uncle needs medical aid."

The second official stared at his tablet and nodded slowly. "That request has already been processed and assessed. Based on data-speculations, deemed not a constructive use of resources." He swiped the page closed and slid the tablet into his breast pocket. "Perhaps if time wasn't being wasted sending us out here, there would be available resources. You should remind your guiding committee of that when we ask for their cooperation."

"We are cooperating," Uncle Niimi said, but so low, I think I was the only one to hear.

I scowl as I remove one of my gloves. I spread my hand out and feel the energy before me. I press against it. At first it resists me, but then my virtual hand passes right through. The beeping stops. The screen shimmers. The letters and numbers of the code smear across the screen like wet ink. They fade and leave behind a blinking cursor.

My hands hang over the keyboard. I can almost see Jack, tapping his finger or marching around the bunker, rolling his eyes and groaning in frustration as I hesitate. Desperation had set me on this path so far from home but after all this, what guarantees did I have from Jack? Would cooperation get what I want from shrugging, smug Jack? I slip on my glove, type in my temporary password and hit enter.

The officials rolled out of town as night fell, before the Tunnel linking our home and the city closed. It felt as if everyone in The Enclave finally took a breath. Jack had avoided it all, hiding with the dead drone. I didn't think secrets were possible in the Enclave, all of us living in each other's lives, but Jack had found an abandoned bunker from before the 'Reconstruction'. There, he had hacked inside the drone, laying out all of its innards, all of its secrets, like a dissected creature.

"They came looking for this, you know," Jack said, gesturing toward the bits and pieces left of the drone. "That's all they care about. That and your EMP that made the blackout."

"EMP?"

"Electro-magnetic pulse. You really are a simp."

"Maybe I should have told them you had the drone. Maybe then they would have helped Uncle Niimi."

"Don't be stupid. Now, let's get to work."

The data lays open like a book.

"Alasie, I can't access it," Jack says, in his bossiest tone. "Did you forget how to spell password?"

"I didn't forget."

I swim through the data stream, riding the wave, taking me to places I never knew, into secrets I shouldn't know. I see names and attached to these, numbers, links in a heavy chain reaching around and through all the people here and out toward others who live in enclaves of their own. I target my uncle's name, and find it easily.

All the details of our lives are laid out like a finished puzzle. Account numbers tally our past efforts. Medical paragraphs predict our future. My uncle's future is dismal and decided because of a probability factor which dooms him now. Unless I do something.

Uncle Niimi's cough kept me awake even after it became a quieter wheeze, my worry growing to a nagging pain in the pit of my stomach. I slipped out of the Enclave during curfew, sleeping the electronic locks until I passed through and ghosting the surveillance waves until I wouldn't even be a blip. I subverted the restrictions on Jack's bunker, far more complex than anything the Enclave had to offer. Owning a bit of Jack's swagger, I sat down and waited in his chair.

Jack opened the door and jerked back in surprise. "What? How?"

"I'm ready. Now can we hack into my uncle's data-specs?"

Jack shook his head. "Not from here." He pointed at a drawer.

I tried it but it was locked. I pressed my hand against it, sent out a pulse and the mag-lock released. Inside lay a jump drive, grey, dull and worn, and obviously very old.

I move the cursor until it lies beside the word Rejected. I try to change the entry but it won't let me. I have unlocked the door and walked into the room but I can't affect anything in it.

"Alasie," Jack said. "You screwed up the password. I can't get in."

"Jack, I can see my uncle's records. Tell me what to do."

"Alasie, what's the password?"

"No. Tell me what to do. Tell me or I'm closing it down and walking out of here."

"Are you crazy? We've come all this way and you're going to pull this crap? Listen you freak—"

I ignore the rest. Beside my uncle's name is mine, but I don't want to look. I don't want to know what future has been mapped out for me, the tally of me and all my potential determined by data crunches that hurt as much as they sound. I don't want any sentences to proclaim my fate. Why should they know? I don't even know what I'll do next.

I see another name and follow that line of code. The verdict on Jack's future is just as grim as my uncle's but for completely different reasons. There are graphs and reports, data dissected and rinsed through predictive algorithms. He is condemned for crimes of the future before he can commit them, before he can make another choice.

I grip the jump-drive through my pocket. "What do you want, Jack?"

"I want access. Now, stop messing around."

"I can see it all Jack. I can see your future."

"Listen, Alasie. They want to keep me down in the Enclave when I should be in the advanced stream. They won't let me in. So, fine. I'll buy my own way. We shave these coins and we'll both have what we want."

Maybe Jack was who they said. But maybe Jack was who they decided he'd be. They put all their notes on the board, drew their graphs and came up with the total that Jack would be. Maybe he was the one that was jinxed.

"They'll say it's you, Jack. Because all the data says it's what you'll do."

"Do you want the money for your uncle or not?"

"The money isn't the issue," I say, seeing clearly through the data stream.

The algorithm crunch crouches like a dam, stemming the tide, sifting through the data. I travel against the current and find the source. It's a muddy mess, fouled by faulty logic based on decades of prejudice, poured into a filter encrypted with cheats for some and scams for others. I glance at my watch. Time is running out. I can't clear this debris hidden behind the code. I can't reprogram it. I can't fix it for my uncle. But maybe if there are enough ripples, I can break the dam. I take off my gloves.

I lay my hands out toward the servers and plunge in. Rivers of my energy flow through the system; wearing away barriers, winding through locks, flushing the system clean. I feel light-headed; little bits of me dribbling out, droplets of me falling onto wires that sing and jingle, chiming out the truth to everyone.

Weeks later, I sit at my desk and stare out the window as my finger scrolls lazily down the webpage. My gloves lay nearby just in case, but I have not had to use them. My control is my glove.

Uncle Niimi is in the city under treatment, the med-boards unable to turn him away when the information waved out of the data hoard and into everyone's awareness. Of course he still had to wait. The hospitals became overloaded with all the other patients, either denied or delayed treatment and now vindicated. The manipulated data crunching of med-aid had the most immediate response; riots, revolts and demonstrations. The knowledge united people who never knew they had a common cause. The newsfeeds said the affect would be felt for years to come.

Data, free and open, zips through the aether. Free to flow. They don't know how the data stream broke its dam. They don't know what sparked the upheaval.

It was just a pebble.

Splash.

Alternative Apocalypse

Back to Reality

Larry Hodges

"Wake up!" said a blurry voice from somewhere as the silly nightmare of an election went *poof.*

"Whaa?" I mumbled, squinting up into the too-bright room. President Trump...wasn't he...?

"You were having a nightmare," said my wife. "You were rolling around moaning about Mexicans and walls, Muslims, Russians, and someone named Hillary."

I came fully awake as she leaned over me in our bed with that look on her face you never want to see. She was looking at me as if I were one of the unchosen with the little yellow crescents pinned to their shirts—or worse still, a blue donkey. "Who is *Hillary*?"

It had all been so vivid, but now the bad dream was disappearing from my mind like smoke from a luger on a breezy afternoon. An *elected* President Trump, beholden to Congress and the people to get anything done? That would never happen, and there's no way we'd ever bring back elections. It's why we had the Orange Takeover. And Hillary Clinton—wasn't she President Clinton's wife? Didn't she get shot for resisting? A traitor—but she'd almost beaten Trump in the election nightmare. But the details...something about Crooked Hillary, emails, and popular vote...I couldn't remember. None of it had happened. The bad dream disappeared like the Statue of Liberty into the rising New York Harbor. *Poof.*

Not our reality.

"Well?" my wife asked. "*Who's Hillary?*"

"You wouldn't believe it," I said. "Just some loser." I sat up. "What time is it?"

"Time to go to work," she said, staring at me for another moment before brightening. "The White House awaits! And today—we're enacting the Final Solution! *At last!*"

I yawned, showered, drank coffee, and we put on our uniforms with the red arrow crosses on our sleeves— swastikas are so cliché. We practically goose-stepped out to the waiting staff car to take us to our offices near the Oval Office, another dream day beginning as the last memory of an election nightmare disappeared forever.

Poof.

To a Soldier's Mother

J. J. Steinfeld

...Good comprehensible morning, dear lovely woman, good comprehensible morning:

Your son has been killed in battle—
    This is not true...

Your son has been killed in battle—
    Chaotic echoes...
    Empty nausea...
    Death without death...

Your son has been killed in battle—
    All memories fulminate...
    Colloquy with oblivion...
    Endless beginnings...

Your son has been killed in battle—
    Endless endings...
    Sundered tears...
    Sundered sleep...

Your son has been killed in battle—
    Heavy seconds pass
    As do the minutes
    As do the hours
    As do the days
    As do the weeks
    As do the months
    As do the years...

Your son has been killed in battle—
    A lifetime passes heavily...
    Savage screams...
    Savage rages...

J.J. Steinfeld

Your son has been killed in battle—
       Silent utterances...
       Beleaguered steps...
       Hopeless hopes...

Your son has been killed in battle—
       Dark thoughts...
       Darker thoughts...
       Darkest thoughts...

Your son has been killed in battle—
       In which war, my God, in which war?

...Good incomprehensible night, dear lovely woman, good incomprehensible night...

Night is the Forbidden

Jean Graham

When Gordie first said he was gonna do it, I didn't believe him. He was always like that, saying he was gonna do a thing and then not, and I guess I figured him being thirteen and a year younger than me, he wouldn't have the nerve. But then one night right in front of Aunt Gert he says that when he's figured out how to unseal the night door, he's going outside.

Aunt Gert nearly had a stroke on the spot, and said he oughtn't trifle with the Law of God like that, and to get all his "outdoorsiness" out of his system in the daytime when he was supposed to. "And you, Benjamin," she says to me over her nose, "you stop putting ideas like that into his head!"

Well I never put it there, but I can't say I never thought about it myself, going outside after dark, I mean. The grown-ups never give you any good reason for all of that kid stuff about demons and monsters. It's all got something to do with freedom of religion and how we came to New Earth, like the pilgrims, and with the stuff people were doing back on Old Earth that we didn't believe in. It's got something to do with all that, only nobody will tell me exactly what.

I tried unsealing one of the doors once, but I couldn't. Gordie's smarter with mechanical things, though. He got a window unsealed. I never would've thought of it, the way he did it. There was a crack in the wall under this window, and he pushed an ice pick in there over and over till it made a round little hole all the way through to the outside. He plugged it with flour paste, so in the daytime no one would notice. Then he stole all kinds of weird stuff out of the kitchen—"borrowed it," he says. Anyhow, he mixed up this powdery stuff and sprinkled it around outside the window one day when nobody was watching him. Next night we both snuck out of bed and went to the same window, and Gordie had a long, thin stick he'd put in the furnace and lit the tip and shoved the lit end through. Next thing I know, *whoosh*— the window seal curls up just like it's morning. Gordie jammed the stick in it so it couldn't come down again. He says he fooled the little glass eye out there into thinking it was daytime, but I still don't understand how. It didn't matter then though, because the seal was open and Night was looking back at us through the open window.

There were hulking, shadowy things swaying out there— the trees, I realized. I'd seen them a million times through that window in daylight, but now they looked like the monsters God says are supposed to wait for you in the night. Me, I never figured why God would want any truck with monsters, anyhow. I think Aunt Gert and the rest just made all that up to scare little kids. Excepting the grown-ups must be scared of *something*, else why don't they ever go out after dark?

Gordie, he must've thought the same, because he stared out that window with me a long time before he whispered, "See? I knew there weren't any demons." Like he expected them to be standing right there, dripping scales and flicking their forked tongues at us or something.

"Well then," I said, all grown-up like, "let's go out and see if we can find some."

Gordie made a noise in his throat, sort of a stifled cough, and went all stuttery on me. "Let's...let's not. Not t-t-tonight, huh? Tomorrow. I think I'm tired now."

"But you got the seal open *tonight*. What's the deal?"

"Nothing. I'm tired, that's all. I can open it again tomorrow night."

I thought he must've spent so much time planning how to fool that stupid glass eye, he'd never really thought about going outside after he'd done it. So now he was scared—too scared even to move.

"All right," I told him. "You be a baby and go back to bed. I'm going out." And I put one leg over the sill, just to show him I wasn't bluffing. "You coming or not?"

He said "Yeah," but he didn't look so sure. He crawled out after me though, and then hung onto the sill like it could save him if some slobbering thing with three-inch teeth suddenly came hulking around the corner. I didn't really much care that he was scared. I was a little shaky myself, mostly because I had the knots-in-the-pit-of-your-stomach feeling we maybe could get caught any minute. But I wasn't afraid of any monsters. Crap on the monsters. I'd never seen Night before, and I wanted to see it. All of it.

The first thing I noticed that wasn't the way I'd expected was the dark. I mean, it wasn't dark, not like when the light is off in your room and you can't see anything. Out here, I could see everything pretty clear, once I looked at it hard. I guess that was because of the moons. I knew the moons stayed out at night, not like the sun, because I'd heard Grandpa Samuel talk about them and how they lit up the night. They say once, a long time ago, he fell off his horse hunting and knocked himself out. Didn't come home all night, and next day about all he could talk about were those moons. Grandma and the others all said he'd gone loony, and nobody paid much attention to him after that. But he still goes on about the moons, and Aunt Gert and Esther and Eban all shush him just like Grandma used to do.

Standing there by the window, the wind blew cold on us, and I think it spooked Gordie, but I liked it. Demon wind it was, maybe, like could take your soul away, and that was fine with me, too. Anywhere away from here. We both knew we'd get a whipping if we were found out. I guess that made just being there a pretty big thrill all by itself. I hadn't felt that tingly since we both snuck our first drink of liquor out of Uncle Eban's still. I wasn't planning to get sick this time, though.

"Geez," Gordie had hunkered down until he was almost sitting in the scorched little mound of his powder concoction. "Look at the buildings."

I squatted down beside him and was about to say "What of it?" till I looked at the other houses too, and saw what he meant. They weren't the same—nothing at all like in the daytime. They seemed closer together, huddled in a scared circle as if they could reach out for each other at the first sign of something dangerous.

"It's the seals, Gordie. The windows, the doors—they're all covered over for the night, like usual. We just never saw it from the outside."

"Let's go, then. We won't find any demons sitting around here."

Gordie started to stammer some more, but rather than stay there all alone, he followed me out past the Donahue's place and their sealed-up barn, over the wood rail fence and into the corn fields. Well, leastways they used to be corn fields before harvest. They'd get rotated to string beans next. The earth was new-plowed now and scrunched under our feet. Shadows, long and spidery, reached out to clutch at us and that wind kept blowing, fresh and chilly and stinging with a wonderful crisp kind of wetness that it never had in the daylight.

"Look up, Gordie. Look at the sky!" I wanted to shout the words out loud, but in the stillness even my normal voice was almost booming.

"It's all different," Gordie squeaked. He was straining his voice through a craned neck. "It's so black. Where does the sun go?"

For some one smart enough to fake out a glass electric eye, Gordie could be awful stupid. "It sinks into the ocean, you dope. Don't you know anything?"

I guess he didn't, because he stared up at that wide, dark sky like it could drink him, and turned circles round and round till he fell *whump* on his backside from the dizzies.

"What *is* that?" he breathed, still sitting there in the plowed furrows, an overgrown turnip with legs. "God, it's beautiful. It *glitters*."

"Not *it*. *They*. The stars. Didn't you ever hear Grandpa Samuel talk about the stars?"

In both his hands, Gordie had picked up dirt clods, and he was crumbling them through his fingers while he talked. "I guess not," he said.

"I dunno what you wanted to come out at night for then." I plopped down beside him to get a better look at the stars myself. "I've been wanting to get out here to see them ever since I first heard Grandpa Samuel say how they sparkled like sun shining on a snow bank."

I could tell by the pout in his voice that Gordie was irked. "So if you wanted out so bad, why didn't you figure out how to break the seals yourself?"

"Because you did, dope."

I guess he didn't feel much like arguing the point, and the stars were too beautiful to argue under anyhow. So we both just sat hugging our knees and watching the sky without saying anything for a while. Then Gordie looked over at me and whispered, "Listen."

"To what?"

"Don't you hear it? Singing. They're singing."

For a minute I thought he'd gone raving crazy. Then I did listen, and I realized there'd been a sound—a whole bunch of sounds, really—chiming like a million little bells ever since we'd climbed through the window. I'd been so wrapped up in looking that I hadn't even thought to wonder what it was, even though I'd been hearing it right along. The sound was almost eerie, now I listened to it close, and it made me shiver just a little. I crossed my arms to keep Gordie from noticing.

"What singing?" I asked him, and then, edgy-like, "That's not singing, stupid."

"What is it then?"

"How do *I* know? Maybe it's the monsters."

He giggled. "Monsters can't sing. Besides, all I see are stars. Just stars."

"What's making the noise, then?"

"It's them," he decided. "It's the stars singing."

"Yeah," I agreed, and looked at the sky with new awe. "I guess it is."

Star music is the most beautiful sound on New Earth. Even though Grandpa Samuel tried to tell me, much later, that it was only a bunch of bugs making that sound out in the bushes and trees, I never believed him. It made sense the stars should have a music all their own, and besides, I never saw a bug yet that knew how to sing like that. It was the stars all right.

Gordie crumbled another dirt clod, scattering the soil in front of him. "I don't believe there are any demons," he said out loud.

"You don't know that."

"Yes I do. It was some old monster tried to eat your great-grandfather that started it all, so they put it down in a book that nobody could go out after night. The monster crawled off and died a hundred years ago, but no one ever came outside to see if it was gone. They just stayed in there, all sealed in, and made up a lot of demon stories to scare little kids with."

"Yeah. But I bet they still believe it, about the demons. Like their parents told them, and their parents' parents told them. Aunt Esther believes it. I can tell just by the way she talks about 'em; how they're all fire-tongued and bulgy-eyed."

Gordie made a snorting noise.

"Your folks believe it. Mine, too."

"They're all crazy."

We listened to the stars sing for a long time then, and one of the moons crawled down toward the ground and got swallowed up. The stars got so much brighter after that, I couldn't believe this was the same sky I'd looked at so often in the daytime, when it was nothing but a boring bunch of cloudy blue.

After a long time, Gordie said, "If there aren't any more monsters, why should Night still be Forbidden? If there weren't ever any monsters, why'd they put it on the list of the Forbidden to begin with?"

I told him I couldn't guess why, except that Night always was on top of the list of the Forbidden, way higher than lying and stealing and just one notch above something called War that I could never get my folks or Aunt Gert or anybody to explain.

"I'll bet I know," Gordie said suddenly. "I'll bet I know where they keep all the answers hidden."

I knew what he was thinking, because I'd been thinking it too. "In Schlessinger's barn, you mean? I figured that too. That's why they keep it sealed up even in the daytime. Something Forbidden's gotta be in there."

"We can find out. Tomorrow I'll mix up some more powder. Barn's got glass eyes, too."

"Maybe there's a monster inside it." The idea excited me.

"Nah. Not unless it's a dead one. Just his bones, maybe. We'll find out."

"Yeah." I leaned back and was almost lying down across the furrows when I felt Gordie go all stiff and rigid and draw in a breath.

"What is it?" I asked him, and sat up straight to look where he was looking, out across the plowed field into the stand of birch trees. They swayed back and forth and muttered to themselves, all dark and black and shadowy. I didn't see anything else out there, and started to say so, but Gordie shushed me.

"Listen," he hissed. "Something's *moving* out there."

I listened, and there was a kind of rustle and crunching noise from somewhere among the trees. It was getting louder, coming toward us.

Gordie was on his feet and I was halfway up when we saw it come out of the bushes, tall and black and stalking straight at us. We didn't stick around to become some monster's dinner. We made for the fence at a dead run and I swear I could hear my heart thumping louder than both our feet. We were almost to the fence before I realized there were more than four feet tearing up ground on the way there, and something was behind us, running too, and probably reaching out to grab for us. I could even hear it breathing, but I was way too scared to look back, scared I'd miss getting over the fence if I tried. We both hit the wood rails at the same time, but halfway over I saw Gordie jerk backwards just like something had yanked him by the collar. He hollered, or started to, but something strangled it off and I heard him fall, kicking and whimpering, back into the dirt. I'd've hollered myself if I could, only the sound refused to come. I had the sudden stupid idea that if I pinched my backside I could wake up safe in bed and everything would be okay. But it wasn't okay. I got over the fence and landed hard on the other side, scrambling to get up and run again, even if I would be leaving Gordie behind. When I stood up, though, I got a really good look at the "demon," and instead of running I just sat back down in the dirt and let my breath out. I almost wanted to cry.

It was Grandpa Samuel. No scaly, clawed, fire-eyed monster, but Grandpa Samuel with his hand clamped over Gordie's mouth, still trying to shush him, because Gordie had his eyes squinched shut and was fighting for all he was worth.

"Quiet!" I whisper-shouted at him, and climbed back over the fence. "Be quiet, you idiot. It's only Grandpa Samuel!"

Gordie opened his eyes then, and stopped fighting when he saw it was true, though his struggling hadn't been getting him anywhere anyhow. Any demon worth its salt would have gobbled him down a long time before this.

Gordie started stammering again when the hand let go of his mouth. "D-did you follow us?"

Grandpa Samuel chuckled the way grown-ups do when they know something you don't. "I was about t'ask you boys that same question. What are you doin' out here, and better asked, how'd you get here?"

"Gordie fooled the eye," I confessed, and felt more like a tattler than a criminal owning up to his crime. "We opened the seal on the southwest window."

"Hm. That's pretty smart, foolin' the eye. How'd you do that?"

"Made a powder that burns bright enough to fake it out," Gordie answered. Then, rather than explain any more, he asked, "How'd *you* get out?"

"Me? I get out most every night, boy, while you're safe asleep in bed. I keep those eyes all workin'. Didn' you know that? I take care of the windmill, which runs the generator, which runs the lights and seals and eyes. I know right how to turn one off when I want."

Gordie hadn't even heard that last part. "Every night?" he echoed. "You come out every night?" He'd gotten up on his feet, and was brushing the dirt off his dungarees.

"Since when?" I wanted to know. "Since you fell off your horse in the woods?"

"Never fell off no horse. Just made that up to explain why I stayed out. Wanted to see the sun go down all the way and watch the stars come out. But I'd been sneakin' out for a long time before that—since I was younger'n either of you. Ain't nobody else I know of in all that time ever tried it but you. Ain't nobody else ever knew *I* did—till now. We ain't gonna tell on each other, now are we?"

With a whole new kind of respect for him, Gordie and I both said, "No, sir."

"Do you stay out all night?" I asked him. "All night every night?"

"Not always. Gotta sleep some time y'know. But if I do spend all night out, ain't nobody cares I sleep late next day. I'm old, see, so they don't wonder. You now—with you they'd wonder. Maybe even start to suspect."

"The demons," Gordie piped up. "Did you ever see the demons?"

Grandpa Samuel looked a little like he wasn't so sure how to answer. "No," he said at last. "Can't say as I ever did."

"Then I was right. There aren't any monsters. No monsters at all."

"Hold on there. I never said there weren't none. I said I never seen 'em. There's a difference."

I climbed back on the fence and straddled it. "*Were* there demons once? Didn't you ever see one, not even a long time ago?"

He leaned on the fence beside me, and his voice all of a sudden got sad. "Never did," he said. "But I heard about the worst one from my grandpa. Grandpa's name was Evan Merrill and he was one of the very first colonists. He could still remember Old Earth and how come we left it. Ain't nobody wants to talk about any of that no more. It's what they call Taboo."

Gordie's nose wrinkled. "What's that?"

"It's anything you can't do," I answered. "Like the Forbidden."

"So?" said Gordie. "What's it got to do with demons?"

"Everythin', son. You want I should show you? You sure you really want to know?" I guess both our eyes lit up then, because he said, "All right, come on," and started walking off toward the Schlessinger place. While we trotted along after, he went on talking.

"Demons on Old Earth had lots of names. And when my Grandpa Merrill and the first Donahues and Vincis and Schlessingers and Kams and some others who ain't here no more all come out to New Earth, they made the demons Taboo: the ones named Lie and Steal and Cheat, Deceive and

187

Adulterate and Murder...and War. That was the worst one, that War one. They say it come after us. Followed us out into the stars and a long while after we was here, it was still lookin' out to devour us. I reckon it almost did, too, and that's how night got to be Forbidden like it is. That's the 'how come?' you was gonna ask me next, wasn' it?"

We both nodded. I saw Gordie's eyes get big when he saw we were walking straight for Schlessinger's barn, the one the seals stayed on all day and night to keep anyone from going in. Grandpa Samuel knew how to get in, though. He used a key to open up a little box on the barn wall and the seal on the main door rolled straight up and the lights went on inside, shining bright through the cracks in the door.

"What's in there?" Gordie asked, all breathless and scared.

"Ain't nothin' to be afraid of." There was that chuckle again. "Then too, maybe it is. Come on, come on. You won't learn nothin' standin' out here."

First thing I noticed about the inside was whitewashed walls, all bright and gleaming—not like the inside of a barn ought to be. There weren't any animals, or hay; not even any stalls or lofts to put them in. And no tack or harness hanging on the walls like in a real barn—just some wire and a few tools hung up beside the gray squatty thing that Grandpa Samuel called the generator. It made all the power work. That was interesting, I guess, but we didn't spend much time looking at it, because there was another machine in Schlessinger's barn, and it was a lot bigger and a whole lot more interesting.

It was more than twice as tall as us, and so long it almost filled up the whole back half of the barn. It had flat, painted metal sides and a domed glass whatsit on top, and there were rust-speckled silver letters on its nose. They said, "Leviathan." I couldn't remember where, but I'd seen that word before.

"I don't suppose," Grandpa Samuel mused, "you'd likely believe me if I told you 'tweren't nothin' but a fancy plow."

"A *plow?*" Gordie and I said it both together, with just the same sort of squeakiness in our voices. I said it over again, though, because I couldn't figure how the wood-carved plows our horses pulled and this thing could ever be remotely related.

"Well, I said a *fancy* plow. Used t'call 'em agro-cultivators, which was just another highbrow word for tractor, which is what they was called before that. Time was we had a whole flock of 'em, crawlin' up'n' down hills like a lot of overgrowed bugs. I hear tell you could plow acres with 'em in less'n a day. That was just a little before my time, though. Can't say I ever did see one movin'."

"It moved?" Gordie said. "How? No horse could pull it. It's way too big."

"Didn' need no horse. Used to run 'em on whatcha call 'chemical fuel.' Used t'get that from the supply ships, till they didn't come no more. My grandpa and the others tried to make their own fuel then, but it didn' work so good. So mostly the tractors got parked in the barnyards, an' we learned how to do things primitive-like. They was all still out there by the time I come along. Whole barnyard full o' Leviathans. I can remember playin' on 'em."

Gordie's finger traced part of the blue and white pattern on the tractor's side and came away dusty. "What happened to them?"

"And the ships," I added. "What happened to the ships?"

"I was comin' to that. Now I've showed her to you, what say we go back outside?"

Reluctant, we followed him out, and while he reset the seal, I remembered where I'd seen the tractor's name. It was in Aunt Gert's Bible, and she'd told me it meant a terrible beast, a monster like the ones living out in the dark. I wondered if the tractors were really Aunt Gert's demons. Maybe now we could go home and tell her there weren't any more running loose to be afraid of.

"Guess I really hadn't ought to be tellin' ya," Grandpa Samuel was saying. "Because once you know, there's no un-knowin'. But I don't figure no harm's in it. There's only the one tractor left, and it ain't got no fuel."

I didn't know what he meant by that, but it didn't matter to me just then, because we were back out under the stars, and I stared up at them so long while I was walking that I ran smack into the Schlessinger's fence and nearly did a nose dive over it. Nobody seemed to notice, luckily.

"There weren't ever any *real* monsters, were there?" I heard Gordie asking as I disentangled myself from the fence rails.

Grandpa Samuel sat on the top rail next to me. "War was real enough," he said. "It come out here after us, so I reckon it musta been real. Don't remember a lot about that the first time it happened. But I was here when it came again. Musta been around eight years old. We hadn't had no supply ships in longer'n that. Guess folks thought war was all over and everybody dead and maybe Old Earth wasn' even there anymore. But another ship did come."

"A ship," Gordie echoed. "A *space* ship?"

"Starship, they called it. And it looked like a star, too. You could see it move across the sky at night, and when the little ships left it to fly down, you could see them, too."

Night, my head whispered back to me. He said you could see it move across the sky *at night.* Aunt Gert never told us the truth. She said Night always *was* part of the Forbidden.

I didn't realize I'd said part of that out loud until Grandpa Samuel answered me. "Far back as she can remember, it was. You forget I'm the oldest one around here. People want to forget what I know, so they figure I'm crazy. Makes it a whole lot easier for 'em."

"The people in the ships," Gordie said, impatient as ever, "what'd they want?"

"*Us,* I hear tell. Wanted folks to go off'n' help fight their war for 'em, cause it'd gone on so long I guess they was short of people to kill off. My grandpa told 'em no, and said that spoke for ever'one, and he figured it was so. Only it wasn' so. Lots of young men here listened real good 'n' hard to what those starship fellas had t' say, all about flyin' up there between the stars and doin' their part for the human race and some other patriotic hogwash. They said their war'd come too close to ignore now—too close to hide from, 'cause all you'd have to do was look up at the sky some uncloudy night and you'd see it up there. You'd see the stars move, the stars that were really ships. And sometimes you could see a bright flash of light and a fireball that'd go spinnin' off into nowhere. When we saw all that, they said, we'd want to go.

"Well there were some young fellas did wanna go, only they didn' dare volunteer right there. So the starship warriors said they'd leave us fuel and supplies and anything else we needed, and maybe when we used it, we'd remember who gave it to us and maybe be a little ashamed of ourselves. Made my grandpa pretty mad, that last part. He took their fuel, though, and he never figured he owed 'em diddly squat for it, either."

"Space ships," Gordie muttered, not absorbing half of what was being said. "Real space ships."

I watched the stars glitter down at me and looked hard for one that moved. "They're all holding pretty still," I said, disappointed.

"Ain't seen one move for near fifty years myself. Oh, little'ns skitter cross the sky ever now'n' then. Ain't the same thing. Back then, you could see the whole sky lit up with 'em, night after night. And those young men I told you listened so close, they watched and they *did* feel ashamed and pretty soon, they wanted to go and find out what flyin' among the stars was like for themselves."

"I'd like to go," sighed Gordie. "I'd like to find out, too."

"Yeah," said Grandpa Samuel a little sadly. "So'd my Pa. And quite a few others. Wasn' much they could do about it though, till one night one of them fireballs went down in Kams' wheat field. They all run out to put the fire out and found out it'd mostly already gone out by itself. All there was left was a burned up space ship in a big charred hole. They buried what was left of her crew, and then they took apart the ship—told everyone else it was for parts to try and fix the tractors, 'cause even with the new fuel we couldn' get most of 'em to run. They'd sat there too many years, I guess.

"So they was smart, these boys. A little too smart, maybe. They took apart the tractors, most of 'em, and built 'em back to look an awful lot like the burned up space ship might've looked before it was burnt. Grandpa Merrill, he figured out what they was doin' and I guess there was a pretty terrible row. But in the end, they went—took their new-built space ships with the fuel the starshippers gave 'em and flew away to join the war. My Pa went with 'em. And more went after that, one by one, soon as they could rebuild a Leviathan and go. Every night the stars moved more and more, and flashed and burned and spiraled down. Just about the last of our young men built ships and left, and nothin' anybody ever tried could stop 'em. Nobody ever came back. Not even one. Grandpa Merrill used to tell about that and cry when he told it, how none of 'em come back."

"But I don't understand," I told him, "how that explains the seals and the eyes and Night being Forbidden."

"Explains it pretty clear, you think about it." Grandpa Samuel smiled at me and suddenly he didn't look half as old as I'd always thought. "You can't go chasin' after what you can't see, boy. My grandpa and the others figured that out soon enough. Had a few tricks of their own left over. Right there in Schlessinger's barn, they'd stashed what was left of the ship *they* come on all those years before. They took apart just about ever' last tractor left, and with all them parts, they built the eyes and the seals and fixed it so no one could watch the war. And just to be extra sure, they burned what was left of the Leviathans—all except one. That one Grandpa Merrill locked away in the barn because he said it was a sin to destroy your own tech-no-lo-gy. That's a big word means 'smarts.' He figured someday the tractor'd get used again for its real purpose. Me, I always hoped I could maybe charge it up somehow with the generator. Only I just never could figure out how."

"Let me try," Gordie begged. "I could figure it, Grandpa Samuel. I know I could."

"Maybe someday," was all the answer he got. "Ain't you boys plannin' on any sleep tonight?"

I objected to that. "Sleep? Who could sleep? Tell us more about the war, Grandpa Samuel. What was it exactly, and why did it happen?"

He shrugged. "Got no answer to that. Don't know nobody ever knew the answer. Anyway, now there's no more war— maybe no more Old Earth either, or if there is they forgot about us a long time since. The stars don't move nowadays, and nobody remembers how to build space ships any more.

Since nobody knows that, though, or wants to, Night just goes on bein' Forbidden."

"I'm gonna go," Gordie said to the stars. "Someday, when I've figured it out, I'm gonna go."

I don't know why, but I believed him. And even though Grandpa Samuel seemed to get a little miffed at that and made us go back inside to bed, we've gone back out most every night since then and watched the stars with him. Maybe one day we'll get to see them move. We've been in Schlessinger's barn again, too, and got to know the tractor better. Gordie wants to know all there is to know about Leviathan, and about space ships too. He says once he knows enough about a thing, it shouldn't be so hard to build it. Soon as we can, we'll get Grandpa Samuel to tell us what one looks like. Then we'll build a space ship of our own.

We can do it. I know we can.

Alternative Apocalypse

Releasing the Tigers

Sandy Parsons

Bliss spread the zoo map over the steering wheel. A tremor of excitement pulsed through her as she traced her finger along the path to the tiger cage. After the last zoo, she needed this one. A memory bubbled up, and she suppressed it before the words conjured a face. *Compelled to act.* That was how Coach had described her in the recommendation letter. Bliss counted nine days since she'd first seen Leah's message. Unless a tiger had a source of food, the odds were tipping the wrong way. With a sigh she folded up the map and dropped the truck into gear.

The smell of rotting meat told Bliss where the supermarket was before her eyes did, but she had learned that hunger superseded smell. After parking her car next to a black sports car, she smeared Vicks vapor rub above her lip, and tied a bandana around her face, old-west-gangster style. With the tire iron weighing down her pants and the flashlight in her hand, she went inside. She walked past snack displays and checkout stands, pocketing snack bars.

Bliss gasped when she saw another person. He was facing away from her, trailing two fingers along the items on the shelf. He grabbed a can of coconut milk and cocked his head to the side. Shrugging, he slid a can opener from his jacket pocket and carved opposing triangles into its metal skin. He drank, head back, body swaying in wrinkled Armani pants, enough gold chains to bend him sideways.

The instant he saw her he tossed the can away, spreading bluish liquid over the lower shelves. He yanked a pistol from his pocket, holding it sideways, but the effect was lost by his trembling hand. No one had ever pointed a gun at Bliss, but her first thought was, *are there leaves in my hair?* He waved the gun erratically in her direction, jerking his head in quick little nods, as if he were trying to convey something to her, some very important signal. Still holding the flashlight, she slowly moved her hands over her head. "It's okay. I'm not going to hurt you."

"Well, duh. I'm the one with the Magnum." In spite of the bravado, the gun trembled, and when she lowered her arms he put the gun away. "You ain't sick?"

Bliss shook her head, unable to keep from grinning. Relief from not having the gun trained on her, followed by a quick desire to hug him. And she would have done it, too, if her knees hadn't turned to noodles. *Another person, alive!*

He smiled too. "Most people go toes up after three days." He turned away, and for a split second Bliss thought he was leaving, but then she saw his hand dart to his face.

"I know what you mean. I saw a couple of kids a few days ago. I tried to follow them, but I couldn't find them. Eventually I gave up. You know, because of the tigers."

"You were chased by tigers?"

"Well, no, er, yes. Just the one. After I let it out."

He scrunched his eyebrows.

"You know, like Leah's been saying. The only thing you can pick up on any TV or radio station. Well, besides some Russian stuff."

He raised and lowered his shoulders. "That was Russian? I thought it was Chinese. Anyways, I don't know Leah. She a friend of yours?"

How could he not have heard Leah? "She's the one broadcasting on every working satellite feed. That's how I learned about the tigers being immune."

The boy pulled back his chin. "You gonna drink tiger blood?"

"What? No. Look, let's start over. My name is Bliss." She held out her hand.

The boy looked at it, then, like a lost toddler whose mother had just been produced, clutched her to his chest and head-butted her shoulder.

Bliss dropped the flashlight and placed her arms around him. He didn't seem particularly clean, but the scent of his neck was like hot biscuits, and she pulled him closer, squeezing away loneliness. They stood that way for a long time, echoing the stillness of the world around them. "I'm Tic," the boy said eventually, his voice muffled by her armpit.

Eventually he pulled back, but left his hands on her upper arms, as if holding her in place. Both of their faces were streaked with tears. "Let me show you something. You're gonna love it."

"Food first. I haven't eaten since this morning."

"Alright, but let's get it to go."

They gathered soda and canned corn, a couple of tired apples (Bliss found the apples. Tic just watched her pick through the produce section while shoveling handfuls of M&Ms into his mouth).

Bliss's SUV was so full there was no room for Tic to sit. She suggested he follow her in the black sports car, a Viper, which she correctly assumed was his. He shook his head and crossed his arms. "What's so important in there anyway? Soccer balls, some dresses, a cake mixer? You can get this crap anywhere."

"Those are volleyballs." She didn't want to explain her shopping spree, or how she'd filled the SUV with volleyballs, some latent stockpiling gene overwhelming her senses, until she realized the indubitable fact that volleyball was not a sport for one. "I've been gathering stuff I need and I don't want to have to go looking for replacements when it's all right there."

"What do you need volleyballs for?"

She shook her head and rolled her eyes, as if it were the stupidest question he could ask. "Fine, we'll take your car. Stop with the third degree."

Tic stuck out his bottom lip as he watched her moving stuff around to get her tiger-freeing equipment out. "That stuff's not going to fit in the Viper."

She held up her hands in exasperation.

"Okay, we'll take the SUV, but I'm driving," he said. But after climbing in and staring out the windshield, he climbed over to the passenger's seat.

Bliss drove with the map in her lap, trying to concentrate on avoiding cars and trash in the road, while Tic rambled on incessantly. "So tell me about these tigers. And what was her name? Leah?" His voice tapered off, and he turned his head as if suddenly interested in the scenery outside. "I thought I was the only one left."

"Leah, is a scientist or something. The first time I saw her was on one of those big screen advertising TVs. Her message repeats. Tigers don't get, you know, the virus. Great for them, except for the ones in zoos. She listed a bunch of zoos, so that anyone left alive can go let them out."

"Why?"

"What do you mean 'why'?" A momentary vision of him splay-legged on the side of the road came to her.

"What if it hurts you?"

Bliss had gone over this scenario in her mind. She had a gun and, although she'd never fired one before, she had it loaded and ready. Like her volleyball drills, she imagined aiming, pulling the trigger. She practiced jabbing with a knife. Save the tiger, but not at any cost.

"Hey? You alright?"

Bliss swerved, then got the SUV back onto the road. "It's like this. The bug killed almost everyone, including animals. So if something survived that, don't you think it should be given a chance?" Tic opened his mouth to speak but Bliss kept on. "I've already set two tigers free, and yeah, it wasn't easy. Okay, okay, I'm done, what is it you're trying so hard to tell me?"

"Can we stop soon? I have to pee."

Tic insisted they share a room at the deserted Marriott. He spread his 'dinner' across his bed. The scent of sugar and chocolate permeated the room, competing with their overripe body odor. Memories of Halloweens past washed over her as she watched him peruse his booty, and a sob escaped her.

"What?" Tic was up off the bed, hands reaching out to her. "I'll share. Really."

She waved him away, even though a part of her wanted to hug him for that sudden bit of compassion. "I was thinking about my parents."

Tic nodded, solemnly. He finished off a candy bar and wiped his hands on the sides of the bed. "Bliss?"

"Yeah?"

"I don't wanna do it. What if the tiger kills you? Or both of us. Why don't we just go back to where you saw those kids you said you saw? We really should be looking for other people."

"I know it sounds weird. And maybe I'm wrong. But I'm not stopping. I don't know if those kids were real or just a figment of my imagination." This was mostly a lie, and she didn't want to lie to Tic, so she stopped talking.

Tic made an exaggerated sigh. "Okay then, I guess. I'll help you this time. But after tomorrow I can't promise anything."

"I'm glad we found each other, Tic."

She dimmed the light and Tic yawned wide, a silhouette in the dark. Bliss yawned too, and then snuggled into the covers. She dreamed that she was back in school, still flush from the excitement of learning about her volleyball scholarship, and everything was the same, except now Tic was there and he kept hiding her volleyballs.

Without the benefit of a weather forecast, Bliss and Tic hadn't anticipated the next morning would be so cold and damp. They had to stop at the zoo's gift shop and pick up sweatshirts. "Souvenirs, great," said Tic, pulling his head through the neck and readjusting his layers of gold chains.

"You might want to ditch the bling. They're gonna throw off your balance."

"Girl, you don't mess with a player's chains."

Bliss rolled her eyes and checked her gear. "Fine. You can tell it to the tiger. I believe they're attracted to shiny things." She shouldered her pack and headed toward the big cat section. When Tic caught up to her, she noticed he was bling-free.

Like the other zoos Bliss had entered, this one was silent, smelly, and sad. There were plenty of bugs, however, and more than once she had to stifle a scream when some moving shadow skittered away from her footsteps. Tic, spooked, fired a shot from his ridiculously large pistol at a mass of cockroaches, sending them scattering. Bliss did scream then. When she was sure her heart wasn't going to jump out of her chest she hissed, "Put that thing away before you shoot yourself, or worse, me."

"Wait, did you hear that?"

"No my ears are still ring—"

Tic cut her off with a slashing motion of his hand.

Bliss was about to rebuff Tic, but then she heard it too. The unmistakable roar. They shared one brief glance before taking off up the slope.

Tic, no longer hindered by his baubles and pack, reached the top of the hill before Bliss. "I see it," he said, between breaths. "You were right. We gotta save it."

Bliss swung her pack to the ground and removed a pair of high resolution binoculars. "Don't get your panties in a wad. Hmm. You know, this tiger doesn't look all that weak." She panned over the tiger enclosure. There was a carcass of something, something big, striped. And not far from that, the remains of a bird. She handed the binoculars to Tic. "This complicates things."

Tic wrung the focusing on the binoculars. "Can't we just swing open the door and run away?"

Bliss snatched the binoculars from Tic and threw them into the bag. "Sure, just like ding dong ditch. Maybe we can set fire to a paper bag of dog poo for the tiger to step in while we're at it. Sheesh."

"Well excuse me. I must have cut school the day they taught us how to let tigers out of cages."

Bliss kicked at a sign depicting a pointing monkey on the back of a rhinoceros. "I need to think about this."

Tic chewed a finger earnestly. Finally, exasperated, he asked, "What's the plan?"

Bliss walked to the ledge which demarcated the enclosure. "Most of these areas are natural barricades, you know, like this trench. I've been using wire cutters on the fence and then putting long planks over the trench, creating a bridge."

"Hmph, low tech. How do you know it worked? Did you see the tiger use the planks to cross?"

Bliss thought about the second tiger, the one that had looked so emaciated and lethargic that she'd thought for sure it would die in spite of her efforts, but crossed the makeshift bridge in two elegant leaps. Looking at Tic now, so earnest, and yet so skittish, she only said, "I leave a large amount of tiger chow by the opening."

"Tiger chow." He giggled. "What the hell?"

"Really. Zoos have chow for every kind of animal. It's mostly corn I think, but probably has some vitamins and stuff. I'll show you."

"If that tiger makes it up the embankment before we get back to the car, we'll both end up tiger chow."

They loaded the SUV with a tub of tiger chow, and found a wooden sign, warped but long enough to reach across the trench. Predictably, Tic grumbled, while they strapped it to the roof with bungee cord.

Now that everything was in place, Bliss was antsy to get it over with. But Tic was hungry, so they ate a lunch of zoo crackers and chips with warm soda. "Could be our last meal," he said stoically, biting the head off a zebra.

Bliss shrugged and brushed Doritos crumbs from her sweatshirt, leaving orange streaks. She pulled it off and threw it in the trash. "Finished yet?"

"Do you think it's forgot about us? We could wait a while, watch it, maybe it'll fall asleep."

"No. Come on now. We're wasting time."

Tic snorted. "All we got is time. If we wanted we could wait until that tiger gets weaker?"

"That would be cruel. Besides, there are still more zoos between here and California, and that means more tigers. They might not be so lucky to have cellmates or birds to eat."

Tic swept the remains of his lunch to the ground. "More tigers for you maybe. But I'm done after this. I'm gonna look for *people.*"

Tic drove while Bliss looked for a good spot along the fence of the tiger enclosure. After a few minutes, she indicated for him to stop. The metallic thud of the door echoed around the entire park and Tic winced.

Bliss picked up the wire cutters and slid out.

The tiger was nowhere in sight. Bliss made quick little snips with the cutters. After a moment her concentration was broken by a rustling of brush. She jumped to her feet, brandishing the wire cutters two-handed in front of her.

"Don't hit me, sheesh."

"Tic, go back to the rig."

"I thought I could set the food up."

She wanted to scream, but took a deep breath instead. "Go unstrap the sign. We're going to have to work fast before the tiger smells that food."

"I was just trying to help," he said, a little bit louder than the required whisper.

She shook her head as she watched to make sure he was following her directions before returning to clipping and pulling back the mesh fence. She was almost done when she had the prickling sensation of being watched. Her first inclination was anger that Tic had come back. She turned around to admonish him, but stopped short. Tic was at the SUV, his back to her. But the sensation of being watched remained. Particularly odd, in the empty world.

She turned, slowly, knees bent, heart hammering.

And there it was. Somehow the tiger had managed to cross the trench and was sitting behind a scraggly bush, gazing at her. It blinked, then turned its head and yawned.

Bliss set the cutters down and took a step backward. On her second step, the tiger turned back to her and stood up. She began walking backwards, wanting to signal Tic but too afraid to take her eyes from the big cat.

With languorous movements the tiger padded closer. To her left and behind her she heard Tic laugh and the heartbreaking sound of his footsteps growing closer.

"Why are you standing like that?" He was now in her peripheral vision. "I'm going to see if I can see where that ti..." He had passed her, and was now in between her and the tiger. "Hey, what?" His voice went up an octave. "I thought you said it couldn't cross the moat. Bliss?"

The tiger sank back on its haunches, looking from person to person. "Bliss, shit, shit, shit. What the hell. Shit."

"Tic, don't make any sudden movements. Come toward me, slowly."

As soon as Tic lifted his foot, the tiger stood up and resumed its leisurely trajectory. In less than a second it would pounce.

Bliss knew she had to act fast. She took two giant steps to place herself between cat and boy. The tiger altered its course effortlessly, and swung a tremendous paw outward. Bliss had spent years honing her reflexes, and jerked away, but claws caught her shirt and she could feel its tendons stretching as it tugged. For an instant she felt like a ragdoll beneath the immense strength. The polyblend jersey ripped and she overbalanced, falling on her butt. Although she was on the ground and vulnerable, the tiger growled and turned back toward Tic.

Bliss clamored to a crouch, laced her fingers together, making a flat plane of the length of her thumbs. She ran and dove low, sweeping upward with her outstretched arms and made solid contact with whatever passed for a tiger's chin. Its eyes squeezed shut and its mouth formed a grimace, rolling backward, stripes akimbo. It landed on splayed paws, and leveled its gaze at Bliss, who was still prone. It wobbled its great furry head at her, as if to say, *what was that?*

"Run!" She shouted at Tic and then promptly jumped up, following her own advice. She and Tic reached the SUV simultaneously. Bliss swung her legs under the steering wheel and turned the ignition. Its roar was as reassuring as the tiger's was frightening. In a panic she drove forward at an alarming speed, but the SUV was facing the enclosure and she rammed the fence.

She flung the gearshift into reverse and gunned the engine. The sign, no longer bungeed to the roof, slid and did a merry triple bounce off the fence before slamming to the ground. The tiger had stopped shaking its head and darted at the SUV. Bliss swerved to miss it, and drove in reverse at top speed, all the way down the path to the crossroads, serpentining wildly the whole way. She altered course with a double-fisted rotation of the wheel and laid rubber all the way to the gate.

When her hands started shaking too much to hold the wheel, Bliss put the SUV into park and pressed her forehead into the steering wheel. She hadn't dared to look at Tic, and she still couldn't quite do so now, but said, between sobs, "I'm sorry Tic, I'm so sorry. It won't, I mean I won't let it happen again."

"Girl, that was straight up skreet."

"What?" Bliss lifted her head, but Tic kept on talking.

"You wailed on that tiger, man." He stopped long enough to chortle loudly, dancing in his seat. "Woot! I am jacked. And we did it, too. We set that mother free. After we showed him who was boss, I mean."

Bliss smiled, but only with one side of her mouth. Her arms had stopped shaking, and she took her hands off the steering wheel and clenched and unclenched them. "Okay, so we're cool then, I guess. I'll drop you off wherever you want."

"Yeah we're cool. But you ain't gettin' rid of me, no sir. We got tigers to free, girl. Oh, and then Leah. We have got to find that girl, and anybody else with a radio or whatever, 'cause there ain't no way this story is staying down. Drive on!" And he leaned over and pressed the horn, two quick honks.

Bliss laughed, nodded, swallowed hard, nodded again. "Okay. Hey, have you ever played volleyball?"

Dancing on the Edge of Eternity

D. S. Ullery

"Damn."

The word was a murmur on Skyler's lips. A numbing coldness settled over him, creating a disconnect between his body and mind. What he was feeling wasn't surprise as much as the deadening solidity of hard facts.

There it was, registered on the Geiger counter they'd found in the bunker the second day. There was no more guessing, no hunches or dread. Just a new reality, permanently etched by the quiver of a needle.

Somehow, a lethal amount of radiation had penetrated their living space. They were all going to die.

Not all at once. Maybe not even for a few weeks. There was precedent for assuming the latter. The colony of survivors he'd managed to initially contact through the in-house shortwave they'd discovered down here had stayed in touch for months. It hadn't been until after Independence Day that the man broadcasting back had informed Skyler of their predicament.

"The children have already begun to succumb," his contact Joey had said. "We have a veterinarian and a nursing intern here and, while neither claims to be an expert on the matter, they're pretty well agreed it's radiation sickness."

Over the course of the next few weeks, Skyler had listened with increasing despair as Joey deteriorated. The fact he could only hear the degradation of the other man's health somehow made it worse. In this dark time, when it seemed humankind was breathing its last, the human voice was the final conduit anyone really had to connect them to other people. The sound of speech emerging from the speaker had taken on an almost divine quality. It was a psychological life preserver, the only remaining avenue for maintaining any sense of community in a world where outdoors travel had been rendered a death sentence.

The dilution in vocal strength. The increase in long, wheezing gasps. The coughing fits. All were evident in ghastly detail. He thought he'd known how to truly listen earlier in his life, but he'd been a novice. Over the past few months, he'd grown so aurally attuned as to pick up on every minute sound issuing from the receiver. He'd even gotten to the point of being able to perceive the low static hum the radio produced just before a broadcast came through from as far away as the outer hall. Skyler supposed it was similar to how the blind developed keener senses when their sight failed.

The broadcasts had dwindled, eventually falling silent at the end of July. He'd made a few half-hearted attempts to raise someone since, but the sick feeling he'd had when greeted by static told the whole story. Joseph "Joey" Lerner, Lerner's family and the four *other* families (who had managed to survive the global cataclysm together) had perished beneath the pervasive onslaught of invisible death.

And now that same enemy had come for Skyler and his own.

Which has been par for the course, he thought bitterly.

It was a sour truth, but valid. One thing Skyler had quickly learned was how much worse things could get when rule of law broke down.

His family had witnessed the brutality of human nature literal minutes after the attacks had begun, even as air raid sirens screamed the death cry of civilization. While terrified television personalities delivered panicked warnings to seek shelter, Skyler's neighbor had arrived at his front door. John Beckman had offered the Lendonberg clan safe haven in the efficiently prepared, subterranean bunker he'd had constructed years earlier.

The thought of John prompted a powerful burst of grief, and Skyler was surprised to find himself struggling against fresh tears. The memory of that terrible morning still haunted him

The two men had grown close when, several years earlier, Skyler (who taught creative writing at the local high school) had John's son in his class. Under his guidance, the boy demonstrated a genuine talent. Encouraged and inspired by a teacher who was making an investment in him, the teen had eventually submitted and successfully published his first short story.

Skyler and John had been close friends since. Though their politics might be different, they shared a mutual respect. Skyler had been deeply moved to discover his family had a standing invitation to accompany the Beckmans should the need for the bunker arise.

The men who had accosted them on the way to the shelter that terrible day had been merciless as they gunned John and his family down. Skyler had barely managed to enter the access codes John had given him months earlier, ushering his family inside just as the gunmen turned their weapons on them. The last clear image he had of the world topside was of father and son, their bloodied bodies crumpled a few short feet from one another. The boy's eyes had been wide open, staring up at a sky he could no longer see.

Chills ran down Skyler's spine as he recalled with uncomfortable clarity the echo of bullets bouncing off the access hatch as he'd sealed it above him, scrambling after his family down the accompanying ladder. As the hatch had closed, he'd heard the shrill, terrified death scream of one of his friend's murderers as hellfire vaporized him.

They'd found themselves in a short tunnel at the bottom, lit by a string of artificial lights, culminating in the entry to the living quarters. As they'd made their way inside what would be their new home, the world had trembled and gone dark. Skyler had huddled with his wife and child in the blackness, that shriek of horror replaying inside his head.

After what had seemed like days (surprisingly, only a matter of hours), emergency lighting had kicked in, and they'd decided to move about to investigate their surroundings. There was enough water and canned goods to last for several years. Further exploration revealed a back room equipped with a small generator and several large, metal, drums of gasoline. The generator powered regular interior lighting, as well as grow lamps for plants and the radio array. An exhaust tube plunged into the concrete foundation, preventing carbon monoxide poisoning by presumably expelling toxic fumes.

A filtration system had been installed which recycled and freshened the air. There was even a system for producing electrical current by turning a wheel and charging a battery which stored the energy in panels. It had been installed in case the generator failed.

The communications console Skyler had been manning for so many weeks was situated in a smaller room, next to the makeshift greenhouse.

John hadn't missed a trick, it seemed.

And the man was gone, along with his family, murdered scant yards from the entrance to the place. Now the counter serving as their fallout warning was delivering the frightening news: Their haven was no longer safe.

There in the communications room with the forever silent radio, Skyler openly wept.

✳✳✳

Upon entering the bunker's common area, he noted his wife had fallen asleep on the sofa John had installed. The room was designed much the way a standard living room would be: The sofa facing a television set up (no broadcasts to pick up, of course, but there was a sizable library of movies and music to play, all stored digitally on protected flash drives which could be plugged into the TV), both separated by a small coffee table. In the corner, a standing lamp cast a warm, amber glow. Under normal circumstances, it would seem cozy. The idea (so Skyler had been informed by his late neighbor) was to establish a sense of familiarity. John had reasoned it would help anyone inside cope with the overwhelming reality of what had transpired above.

Madeline was curled up, her legs drawn under her, her face half buried in one of the small throw pillows adorning the sofa. Soft breaths escaped her every few seconds and a smile curled her lips. Skyler's heart ached at the sight of that smile. Only in her dreams could his wife express anything remotely approaching joy these days. During her waking hours, her face remained impassive. As if it were taking all of her energy just to not break down.

Which is probably the truth of it, he thought.

A sudden, blazing anger swelled inside of him, directed at God, the Devil, Man and any other target he could think of. Skyler wasn't sure which was worse—suddenly knowing they were all going to die, or his absolute impotence in the face of that reality.

He considered waking her, then thought better of it. What would be the point? Rousing Madeline now would only pull her from a seemingly benign dream, denying her the only escape she had left. There was little point anyway, he reasoned. All he planned to do was let her know it was time to take the pills.

Skyler shuddered at the thought of the tiny red lock box stashed away in their bedroom. There were six tablets inside, placed there in the event of a worst-case scenario. Specifically, *this* scenario. Three had been intended for John and his family, the others added once he'd decided to invite Skyler and his brood to join them.

"A last ditch solution," John had explained, his tone grim as he revealed to his neighbor the key to the lock box. "If the radiation does somehow get in and it looks as if we're not going to make it, swallowing one of those will allow us to slip out peacefully. You'll go to sleep and never wake up."

Madeline had been adamant the pills be kept somewhere their son wouldn't get to them. Aside from the common area, the communications room and a small restroom, there were four other spaces designed as living quarters. Two would host the respective parents, the other two occupied by the children.

Skyler had suggested they place the box inside one of the two empty rooms. Part of his reasoning had been based on the anticipation they would never truly need the tablets. On some deeper level, though, he knew that wasn't the only factor. He wanted a reason to close off those two rooms for good, so their devastating emptiness wouldn't provide a constant reminder of what had already been lost.

Madeline wasn't having it. If there was any chance their son could wander into the selected room unattended and get his hands on that box, that was an instant deal breaker. She pointed out, with good cause, the boy was likely going to enter his teenage years while still surviving down here. One day he might be tempted to pick the lock on the door of the forbidden room while they were both asleep, just to see what was inside.

Both parents had finally agreed the lock box should be kept in the bedroom they shared. Skyler had decided to keep the key on him at all times. They took the extra step of never telling their son about the box.

Skyler quietly crossed the common area, approaching two similar doors. He carefully opened the one on his left, peeking in on his child. The boy was curled up in his bed, fast asleep. His face was a mask of complete peace. Next to him, a wind-up alarm clock with luminescent hands revealed it was a quarter past midnight. No wonder everyone was asleep.

Trembling, Skyler quietly closed the door, slipping inside the other room. Satisfied he hadn't woken either of them, he made his way to the bed.

He groped at the shadows underneath the bed frame for a few seconds before his fingers found purchase on cool metal. His heart beginning to beat faster, he withdrew the lock box, balancing it on his knees. He slipped his hand in his pocket, extracting a small ring hosting a single key.

It was a dull thing, nothing more than a sliver of tarnished silver. Yet, as innocuous an object as it was, it might as well have been a loaded gun.

Skyler remembered something John had told him one afternoon, as the situation overseas had grown worse and talk of affairs potentially leading to the much dreaded Big One had begun to dominate the media.

"It's inevitable, Skyler," John had said with a calm certainty. "For all of human existence, mankind has been dancing on the edge of eternity. We've courted the Grim Reaper—against our own interests, even—for the entire duration. Every year we come closer to finally tipping the balance and tumbling over that edge.

That's because—despite our so-called civilization, despite all of our culture—we're still just primates. If we can't dominate, we'll settle for the instinctual pleasure of destroying our enemies."

They'd drowned the rest of that rather mordant conversation in some tasty beer that day, and Skyler had, for the most part, put it out of his mind. Staring at the key now, he realized how completely he agreed with the dead man.

A bitter snort escaped him at the thought. It would be folly *not* to believe. With everyone else dead because of the human need to "get them as good as they got us", and his own family staring mortality in the face, there was no other recourse. Life itself had become the confirmation of John's truth.

He made quick work of opening the box and extracting the needed number of tablets. He moved to again secure the box and return it to its dark space beneath the bed, when it occurred to him there was no point. There would be no one left to get at the contents.

Skyler held the three tiny, gray pills in his open palm, regarding them quietly. He felt hollow.

Do you realize, he thought, the emptiness seeming to echo through him, *you may well be holding the end of the human race in your hand? Ladies and gentlemen of the universe, all you elder Gods of Heaven and Hell—presenting Skyler Lendonberg. Age forty. Father of one, husband to Madeline Baker-Lendonberg. The man who rendered the human race extinct.*

For all he knew, it was true. If the radiation was seeping in here and had also taken the members of the colony, it stood to reason the same drama was playing out all across the globe. The three of them might be the last people left.

The sound of his wife stirring on the sofa pulled him out of his grim reverie, and he chided himself for indulging such melodrama. If ever there was a moment requiring his complete, undiminished attention, this was it.

Skyler rose from the bed, palming the tablets and slipping them into his pocket. He braced himself, knowing he had to do this but hating it every step of the way. A while back, when John had explained to him about the pills, his neighbor had offered him an opportunity to glance through a medical journal containing images of people who had suffered fatal radiation sickness. He found himself presently grateful to John for driving the point home. He shivered, combating a surge of nausea as the reality of what his family was facing truly connected for the first time.

Slipping back into the common area, he was surprised to find Madeline awake. She favored him with a sleepy half-smile. A tremor of grief forced his heart to beat faster. Was he really about to do this to someone who could still give him any kind of a smile under these circumstances?

He reminded himself of the pictures from the medical journal. It served to quell the doubts.

"Is Jacob sleeping?" she asked softly.

"Yes," Skyler told her. "I think he's having a good dream. He was smiling."

"Thank god," she answered, shifting on the sofa and stretching her legs. She yawned, reaching over her head, her back curving like a cat's. He watched her, remembering the day he'd proposed. They'd been at a quiet spot by a lake, the place where they'd first met. She'd been wearing nothing fancier than cut-off denim shorts and a midriff tee shirt, but Skyler had thought her to be the most beautiful creature on the planet. Nothing had changed in the years since.

That had been late summer. Since then, he'd come to love the end of the season, as it reminded him of his happiest memory. He'd been presumptuous enough to believe that would never change. Then the world had gone mad, his fond memories another victim of the global catastrophe.

"What are you thinking about?"

The question brought him back to the present. Skyler felt a stab of guilt. Given this was the last conversation he was likely to have with his wife, this was a most inappropriate time for woolgathering. He sat down next her.

"Just life. How, in the middle of this nightmare, we somehow managed to stay together as a family."

"Oh." Whatever interest she might have had was already draining away. The dull, empty look was returning to her eyes.

"Hey, would you like a drink of water?" Skyler asked. "You look a bit thirsty."

"Yeah, that'd be great," Madeline affirmed, at least attempting a smile. She reached out and placed a hand on

Alternative Apocalypse

his cheek. "I know I can't really show it, but I'm glad we're all together too. You're what's been keeping me going."

Skyler leaned in and planted a light peck on her cheek before exiting the room, stepping into the short outer corridor connecting the common area to the communications array. As soon as he was out of her line of vision, he released a breath he hadn't consciously realized he'd been holding. His eyes stung and he swiped at them angrily, willing himself to not cry again.

Further ahead on the left was a small space where they stored the consumables. The door was partially open. No doubt that had been Jacob, forgetting to close it behind him as young children are known to do.

I would have him forget to close doors, not put down toilet seats and never clean up after himself every day for the rest of his life not to have to do this, Skyler thought bitterly.

At first glance, it would seem to anyone not in the know there wasn't enough here to keep a family alive for more than a few weeks. In reality, the floor of the storeroom had a door built into it. Underneath, a short ladder accessed a storage space roughly the same dimensions as the entire bunker. Most of the goods were kept there. How ironic it would likely never be found or used.

Up top, several cases of bottled water were stacked in the corner of the room, next to bags of rations, powdered milk and other items designed to provide necessary nutrition without requiring refrigeration.

The shrink wrap binding the top case had been torn. He rummaged inside of it, grabbing one of the plastic cylinders and unscrewing the top, the plastic ring crackling as he twisted it loose. Skyler slipped one of the pills through the mouth. Once the tablet had disintegrated into a fine cloud, he shook the bottle, mixing it up. The milky quality of the contents quickly cleared. At a casual glance, it looked like a perfectly benign bottle of spring water.

He had started back to the common area when he heard his wife speaking to someone. This was followed in short order by the sleepy tones of a child's voice. Jacob must have awoken and come out to see what was going on.

"*Sky, sweetie,*" Madeline called from the other room, "*Jacob is awake. He says he wants a drink of water. Can you grab a bottle for him as well?*"

"*Sure. Be right there!*" he yelled back.

It all came crashing down on him. The strength went out of Skyler's legs and he sagged, pushing his back against the wall of the storeroom for support. Turning his head to one side, he closed the door behind him and buried the muffled, screaming sobs he could no longer push down in the crook of his arm. His body shook with each violent outburst of horrified misery as it all forced its way out.

Get it together, man, he warned himself. *If you're in here too long, she'll get worried. If she sees you like this, they'll know something's up. Clean up and get on it with. All you can do now is give them a blissful exit.*

The cold reality of this last thought dragged him mercilessly out of his state.

All you can do now is give them a blissful exit.

And that was all there was to it, right?

Skyler dried his eyes and cleaned up his face using the hem of his shirt. He snatched two more bottles of water and quickly went through the same steps for each. He'd decided he would let them drink first, waiting until they drifted off. Then, once he'd confirmed it was done, he would consume his own.

There would be no need for burials, no one to discover what remained or be offended by it.

It would be quick and it would be quiet.

Peaceful.

He stepped into the hall, wondering how it would feel as the dance ended and they plummeted over the edge into eternity.

The Last And Greatest Vision of Saint Ethan The Obscure

P. L. Ruppel

God is a comedian playing to an audience too afraid to laugh.

-Voltaire

Father Jonathan Walsh, the last surviving monk of the Order of Saint Ethan the Obscure, was ninety years old when he visited the Vatican Library. He had worked with his brother monks and sister nuns to produce a small book of keys. And now, in the culmination of lifetimes of work, he was ready to decode the manuscript Ethan Ultimo Apocalypsis, the record of the last and greatest vision of his order's founder.

Ethan of Britain was called the Obscure because he was almost unknown outside a fifty-square-mile radius of a town called Maryloss and because he made all his prophecies using a series of increasingly difficult codes. The old monk had said that his last prophecy was his most accurate. He had also claimed that the code was unbreakable.

At the Vatican, Father Walsh was led to a small climate-controlled room where the fragile document lay. They gave him a pair of cotton gloves and demonstrated how he should handle the pages. They smiled and pointed, but didn't speak, because the old priest was stone deaf.

The manuscript was written in a closely spaced script on pale beige sheets of parchment, the edges crumbled. The margins were filled with faded paintings of angels blowing trumpets with their backsides, mandrakes making love, and naked nymphs sporting with satyrs.

Father Walsh took out an imitation-leather-bound book from his satchel. Its delicate pages were filled with columns of Hebrew, Aramaic, and Roman letters arranged under Arabic and Roman numerals. He also took out a legal pad, a pencil, and an eraser. Within an hour, he had filled two pages of the pad with a Latin translation of the manuscript. He didn't slow down to read, he only transcribed what was in front of him. By the end of the hour, his arthritis was killing him. He sat up very slowly and winced as his joints popped.

When he read what he had decoded, he giggled. He snorted, he chuckled. His joints no longer hurt so much, and he resumed his work and decoded the last page.

When he read the entire piece, he laughed out loud and pounded the desk. A concerned clerk opened the door, fearing the old man was having a seizure. Upon feeling the hand on his shoulder, Father Walsh showed the confused clerk the translation, and the clerk laughed.

They showed it to the Cardinal Librarian and Archivist of the Holy Roman Church, a man who hadn't laughed in forty years. He howled until tears ran down his cheeks and he leaned against the wall for support.

The Cardinal Librarian shared the translation with the Pope. His Holiness giggled and snorted all the way through his next audience in St. Peter's square, where he read the translation in English, Italian, and Spanish. The audience collapsed in gales of laughter and got out their phones to share the Vision online.

The text of Ethan's Vision and the video of the Pope went viral within minutes. The Vision was translated into English, Chinese, French, Swahili, Hindi, Arabic, Russian, and Portuguese. It was funny in all of those languages and to everyone who read it or heard it.

Giggling newscasters read the Vision to their audiences in place of their headline stories. Soldiers read it to each other and stopped shooting. A shouting match on the floor of an Asian parliament collapsed into hysterics when the prime minister read the Vision. The International Space Station crew learned it from the ground crew and laughed so hard that they forgot to hold onto something for stability and floated through the station until the ventilation system washed them up against the bulkheads.

As the number of people laughing increased, the Earth's seismic activity increased exponentially.

Earthquakes erupted first on the Pacific Rim. The ocean reached up and swallowed the coastal cities of the Americas and continued around until the tsunamis and tremors collapsed Tokyo on parties of people hugging each other. The Arabian and Anatolian fault plates snapped and buckled, throwing the last standing antiquities on Jews and Arabs sharing hookahs in Jerusalem. Mount Etna roared to life as the African and Eurasian plates ground together. The Mid-Atlantic Ridge surged and split open. The seas boiled. Yellowstone erupted.

Earth heaved and strained and came apart like a peeled fruit. Within minutes the planet and its orbiting hardware were replaced by a mass of red-hot debris.

Saint Michael the Warrior stood on a reef of Space and Time and viewed the chaos with an un-angelic expression of shock and horror. Someone had failed to inform him of this part of the Divine Plan.

He called Saint Genesius over to him, spread his great warrior's hands over the remains of Earth and said, "What was that all about?"

Genesius, patron of comedians, actors, lawyers, and half a dozen other groups that no longer existed, only chuckled. "Michael, if I have to explain it, it just isn't funny."

Contributors

David Bernard is a native New Englander who hightailed it to South Florida as soon as he was informed that grown-ups can live anywhere they want, and that in spite of opinions to the contrary, he was considered to be an adult. He does still keep an ice scraper by the door, because you never know. His previous works include short stories in anthologies such as *Strangely Funny* (Mystery and Horror, LLC), *Snowbound with Zombies* (Post Mortem Press), *Legacy of the Reanimator* (Chaosium), and *The Shadow over Deathlehem* (Grinning Skull Press).

Rupert McTaggart Brackenbury is a business analyst & public servant. He lives in Wellington, New Zealand with his wife and two sons. News about his writing (and further ramblings) can be found on twitter: @RupertBBare.

Ian Creasey lives in Yorkshire, England. His most recent book is *The Shapes of Strangers*, a collection of science fiction stories, published by NewCon Press. For more information, see his website iancreasey.com.

Andrew Davie received an MFA in creative writing from Adelphi University. He taught English in Macau on a Fulbright Grant. He's also taught English and writing in New York, Hong Kong, and Virginia. In June of 2018, he survived a ruptured brain aneurysm and subarachnoid hemorrhage. Links for his short stories and novella can be found on his website: asdavie.wordpress.com

Tomas Furby is a graduate of UEA's English Literature with Creative Writing BA and has worked in the publishing industry for a decade. He is based in Didcot, UK, and spends his spare hours writing strange stories and weird worlds. In 2018 he won Exeter Writers Short Story Competition and was longlisted in the James White Award. In 2019 he was longlisted for the Bath Short Story Award and shortlisted in the Frome Short Story Competition. His work can be found at tomasfurby.com.

Henry Gasko was born in a displaced persons camp in Yugoslavia after World War Two, raised on a vegetable farm in Canada, and is now living in Australia. He has recently retired from a career in data analysis and medical research. He won the 2018 Sapiens Plurum short story competition, and has had stories published in the anthology "Dreamworks", Australia's *Aurealis* magazine, and in the *SciPhi Journal.*

Michelle F Goddard is an AWADJ (artist with a day job), a musician who has played around the world, and a composer with credits to her name for original songs performed in musicals and films. Her short fiction has been published in Iguana Books' *Blood is Thicker* anthology and *Polar Borealis Magazine*, with work forthcoming from Ulthar Press among others. She is presently working on several short stories and a Science Fiction novel. You can find her at michellefgoddard.wordpress.com.

Debora Godfrey has had stories published in *More Alternative Truths: Stories from the Resistance*, *Alternative Theologies*, and *Alternative Truths III: Endgame*. She is also co-editor for *Alternative Apocalypses*. She's working on a middle grade fantasy series, as well as a crime novel based in space. Debora lives in a modern commune on Bainbridge Island, WA, with a dog, a husband (part time), and a variable number of lawyers.

Jean Graham began making up stories at the age of three, and never stopped. Her work has appeared in magazines such as *Mythic* and *Weirdbook*, and in the anthologies *Time of the Vampires*, *Memento Mori*, and *Killing it Softly 2*, among others. A member of both SFWA and HWA, she resides in San Diego, CA with her husband Chuck, five cats, innumerable dust bunnies, and many, many books.

Contributors

B. Clayton Hackett is an attorney who lives with his wife and two children in South Texas, a place that is becoming more dystopian by the day (even by Texans' standards). He hopes his unlikely work as a calendar model was merely an anomaly and not a portend of some impending apocalypse. He has previously appeared in *Daily Science Fiction.* "The Golden Disks" marks his first publication in an anthology.

Stuart Hardy is a British internet comedian from the Youtube channel *Stubagful* where he makes offbeat and cynical video reviews of TV shows like *Doctor Who*, *Stranger Things*, *Black Mirror* and *Inside Number 9*. He's been writing sci-fi and satire for a very long time but only started taking it seriously in 2016 when the world got noticeably worse.

Philip Harris was born in England but now lives in Canada where he works for a large video game developer. Not content with creating imaginary worlds for a living, he spends his spare time indulging his love of writing. His published books include the *Serial Killer Z* series, the *Leah King* Trilogy and an homage to the old pulp science fiction serials - *Glitch Mitchell and the Unseen Planet*. His short fiction has appeared in numerous anthologies and magazines including *The Jurassic Chronicles*, *Tales from the Canyons of the Damned*, *Bones*, *Uncommon Minds*, *The Anthology of European SF*, and *Peeping Tom*. He has also worked as security for Darth Vader. You can find more details of his work and his blog at http://www.solitarymindset.com.

Larry Hodges is an active member of SFWA with 103 short story sales and four novels, including *When Parallel Lines Meet*, which he co-wrote with Mike Resnick and Lezli Robyn, and *Campaign 2100: Game of Scorpions*, which covers the election for President of Earth in the year 2100. He's a member of Codexwriters, and a graduate of the six-week 2006 Odyssey Writers Workshop, the 2007 Orson Scott Card Literary Boot Camp, the two-week 2008 Taos Toolbox Writers Workshop, and has a bachelor's in math and a master's in journalism. In the world of non-fiction, he has 13 books and over 1800 published articles in over 160 different publications. He's also a professional table tennis coach, and claims to be the best science fiction writer in USA Table Tennis, and the best table tennis player in Science Fiction Writers of America! Visit him at larryhodges.com.

Liam Hogan is a member of the Post Apocalyptic Book Club and loves stories that begin: "The End". London based, his award-winning short story "Ana", appears in *Best of British Science Fiction 2016* (NewCon Press) and "The Dance of a Thousand Cuts" in *Best of British Fantasy 2018*.

With a couple of mouse clicks, you can find out more at: http://happyendingnotguaranteed.blogspot.co.uk or tweet @LiamJHogan.

Daniel M. Kimmel is the 2018 recipient of the Skylark Award, given by the New England Science Fiction Association. He was a finalist for a Hugo Award for "Jar Jar Binks Must Die... and other observations about science fiction movies" and for the Compton Crook Award for best first novel for "Shh! It's a Secret: a novel about Aliens, Hollywood, and the Bartender's Guide". In addition to some two dozen published short stories (including in *Alternative Truths* and *Alternative Truths III: Endgame*), he is the author of the novels *Time on My Hands: My Misadventures in Time Travel* and *Father of the Bride of Frankenstein*.

Brian K. Lowe is a member of the Science Fiction and Fantasy Writers of America (SFWA), with over 40 story publications to his credit. He has also published seven novels, including his trilogy *The Stolen Future*, available from Digital Science Fiction, and the continuing adventures of Nemesis, a 1930s pulp hero. He is currently working on a spin-off novel set in the world of *The Stolen Future*. Look for him on Twitter @brianlowewriter, his blog Graffiti on the Walls of Time (brianklowe.wordpress.com), or at brianklowewriter@aol.com.

Christine Lucas lives in Greece with her husband and a horde of spoiled animals. A retired Air Force officer and mostly self-taught in English, she has had her work appear in several print and online magazines, including *Daily Science Fiction*, *Pseudopod/Artemis Rising 4* and *Nature: Futures*. She was a finalist for the 2017 WSFA award and is currently working on her first novel. Visit her at: http://werecat99.wordpress.com/.

Ugonna-Ora Owoh is a Nigerian poet and model, He is a recipient of a 2018 Young Romantics/Keats Shelley prize, and a 2019 Erbacce Prize. He is a winner of a 2019 Stephen A Dibiase International poetry prize and a 2018 Fowey short story prize. He was a highly commended poet for the 2019 Blue nib Chapbook Contest. His recent poems are on *Confingo Magazine*, *The Malahat Review*, *The Matador Review*, *The Puritan*, *Vassar Review* and elsewhere. He is featured in *Pride Magazine* and **Puerto Del Sol Black Voices** series.

Sandy Parsons writes literary, philosophical, humorous, and speculative fiction. She has studied physics, math, molecular biophysics, and medical science, but only ponders the fundamental nature of reality for fun these days. When not writing, Sandy is an anesthetist and an associate editor at http://escapepod.org/. More information can be found at http://www.sandyparsons.com/

Mike Resnick is the author of 77 novels, more than 280 stories, and 3 screenplays. He has edited 42 anthologies, and currently edits Galaxy's Edge Magazine and Stellar Guild Books. According to *Locus*, Mike is the all-time leading award winner for short fiction. He has won 5 Hugos (from a record 37 nominations), a Nebula, and other major awards in the USA, France, Japan, Spain, Catalonia, Croatia, Poland, and China. He was Guest of Honor at the 2012 Worldcon. His daughter, Laura, is also a science fiction writer, and won the 1993 Campbell Award as Best Newcomer.

James Rowland is a New Zealand-based, British-born writer. His work has previously appeared at *Aurealis*, *Black Dandy* and *Compelling Science Fiction*. When he's not moonlighting as a writer of magical, strange or futuristic stories, he works as an intellectual property lawyer. Besides writing, his hobbies are reading, stand-up comedy, travel, photography, and the sport of kings, cricket. You can find more of his work at his website https://jamesrowlandwriter.wordpress.com.

P. L. Ruppel is a writer and science librarian who lives in the Washington, D.C. suburbs. She works on biomedical database indexes for the federal government. She is a Michigan native who still can't work out why anyone considers forty degrees Fahrenheit "cold."

Melvin Sims lives on a fourth floor walkup in southern Indiana where he is able to gaze out nightly at the giant cross erected across the street, adjacent to an idyllic park where children play and dogs are walked. He lives alone, visited only by the bible bearing folks who would save his soul, given the chance, but seldom accept an offer to join him for a bong hit.

Canadian fiction writer, playwright, and poet, **J.J. Steinfeld** lives on Prince Edward Island, where he is patiently waiting for Godot's arrival and a phone call from Kafka. While waiting, he has published 19 books, including *Would You Hide Me?*, *Misshapenness*, *Identity Dreams and Memory Sounds*, *Madhouses in Heaven, Castles in Hell*, *An Unauthorized Biography of Being*, *Absurdity, Woe Is Me, Glory Be*, and *A Visit to the Kafka Café*. His short stories and poems have appeared in numerous periodicals and anthologies internationally, and over 50 of his one-act plays and a handful of full-length plays have been performed in Canada and the United States.

Mikal Trimm has sold over 50 short stories and 100 poems to numerous venues including *Postscripts*, *Strange Horizons*, *Realms of Fantasy*, and *Ellery Queen's Mystery Magazine*. He lives in a small town outside Austin, TX, where the weather is pleasantly miserable.

Contributors

D. S. Ullery has been published in multiple magazines and anthologies., including *Journals of Horror:Found Fiction; Paying the Ferryman*; *Final Masquerade;* and *Creature Stew.* He is an Affiliate member of the Horror Writers Association and lives in West Palm Beach, FL with a black cat named Jason, who was born on Friday the 13th.

Patrick Winters is a graduate of Illinois College in Jacksonville, IL, where he earned a degree in English Literature and Creative Writing. He has been published in the likes of *Sanitarium Magazine, Deadman's Tome, Trysts of Fate*, and other such titles.

A full list of his previous publications may be found at his author's site, if you are so inclined to know: http://wintersauthor.azurewebsites.net/Publications/List.

Jim Wright is a retired US Navy Chief Warrant Officer and freelance writer. He lives in Florida where he watches American politics in a perpetual state of amused disgust. He's been called the Tool of Satan, but he prefers the title: Satan's Designated Driver. He is the mind behind Stonekettle Station (www.stonekettle.com). You can email him at jim@stonekettle.com. You can follow him on Twitter @stonekettle or you can join the boisterous bunch he hosts on Facebook at Facebook/Stonekettle. Remember to bring brownies and mind the white cat, he bites. Hard.

Jane Yolen has published almost 380 books and has her eyes on the big 4-0-0. Along the way she's won 2 Nebulas, 3 World Fantasy Awards, The Skylark Award, and a Caldecott Medal for her book OWL MOON. At age 80, she is in a band. She was the first woman to give the Andrew Lang Lecture at the University of St Andrews, Scotland, a lecture series that began in the1920's and included talks by both John Buchan and J.R.R. Tolkien among others. She is a SFWA Grand Master, SFPA Grand Master, and a Grand Master of World Fantasy.

You want a minor apocalypse? One of her awards set her good coat on fire.

Thanks Debora, Becky, and Ben,
and all who helped.
It's been a hoot.
Bob B

IF YOU ARE STILL READING? YOU ARE MY HERO.

Manufactured by Amazon.ca
Bolton, ON

23396670R00132